# HIGH HOSTAGE

After the death of her husband, Alix Johnston sets off on what is supposed to be a holiday on the exotic Greek island of Corfu. Hiding out on the island is Cary, her husband's cousin, a notorious financier who is wanted by the police. Alix discovers that his son, Benjamin, is being kept a virtual prisoner on the island. Conscience, loyalty and fear sweep Alix into a smuggling plot filled with intrigue and danger. Drawn deeper into the devious scheme for Benjamin's sake, Alix must ultimately deceive the one man who can help her—and with whom she has fallen in love—and finds herself aiding a murderer in an escape plot that takes her and Benjamin on a dangerous journey through the island mountains where Alix discovers she is the hostage.

# HIGH HOSTAGE

## Anne Worboys

CHIVERS LARGE PRINT
Bath, England

CURLEY LARGE PRINT
Hampton, New Hampshire

**Library of Congress Cataloging-in-Publication Data**

Worboys, Anne.
 High hostage / Anne Worboys.
  p.  cm.
 ISBN 0–7927–2026–1 (lg. print).
 ISBN 0–7927–2025–3 (pbk.: lg. print)
 1. Man–woman relationships—Greece—Crete—Fiction.
 2. Women—Travel—Greece—Crete—Fiction.
 3. Widows—Greece—Crete—Fiction.
 4. Large type books.
[PS3573.O6878H5  1994]                        94–4564
813′.54—dc20                                     CIP

**British Library Cataloguing in Publication Data available**

This Large Print edition is published by Chivers Press, England, and by Curley Large Print, an imprint of Chivers North America, 1994.

Published by arrangement with the author.

U.K. Hardcover  ISBN  0 7451 2253 1
U.K. Softcover   ISBN  0 7451 2261 2
U.S. Hardcover  ISBN  0 7927 2026 1
U.S. Softcover   ISBN  0 7927 2025 3

*Printed in Great Britain*

# CHAPTER ONE

Heathrow was hell as usual. Passengers with large bags were rushing round looking for the trolleys. There was an enormous queue at the Olympic Airways desk and the girl dealing with the tickets had stopped work to talk to an official.

Paul Crispin, glancing idly toward the entrance, saw a tall, pretty girl coming in accompanied by a little white-haired woman walking with the aid of a stick. He watched their progress with interest. The girl wore well-fitting jeans with a wide, studded belt, a cotton crêpe blouse unbuttoned at the throat, and slung over one arm she carried a red jacket. She had one of those smooth, expensive haircuts that were all the rage that year and which made a girl look both boyish and feminine. They had stopped and were looking at the queue in which he stood. Paul straightened and his eyes lit up. Then the girl sighed and the old lady, taking her very determinedly by the arm, hustled her off toward the coffee bar. Paul slid out of the queue and, like a homing pigeon, made for the same door.

'It's terribly kind of you, Aunt Lucilla,' Alix was saying, 'but I am really perfectly all right on my own, and I can't help thinking

1

you ought to be resting that foot.'

'Nonsense, dear,' Lucilla retorted briskly. 'At my age I might as well do what I want to do. There's no point in lying on a sofa extending a useless life.' She paused beside an empty table. 'I'll settle here while you get the coffee.'

Paul waited by the doorway until the old lady was seated, then he sat down at a table near by. He leaned back for a better view of the girl, eyeing her long legs, her neat buttocks, her slim waist, as she inched her way past the sandwiches and croissants and pies towards the cash register. With his expert eyes he had noted immediately that the woman with the stick was here merely to see the girl off. A beautiful girl. A bedworthy girl. And going to Corfu? Alone? The opportunist in him leaped to the fore. There was that Niagara spill of adrenalin shooting with happy familiarity through his veins. He took a packet of cigarettes from his pocket, flipped one out and lit it. The girl crossed the room with effortless grace, a coffee balanced in each hand. He sized her up with practised skill as the two women talked.

'So, I am going to Corfu after all,' Alix was saying with a kind of apprehensive wonder. 'Odd, isn't it, how life turns full circle? Perhaps,' she added, her mouth twisting a little, 'there is punishment for me in this.'

'Alix!' exclaimed her aunt. 'You have got

to stop thinking it's your fault Tim is dead.' And then, more gently: 'I wish I could convince you.'

Lucilla Farrington, Alix's great aunt and guardian, held certain theories regarding Time and Fate. The spirit knew, she believed, the predestined date it was to leave the body. 'I think you would be a whole lot more resigned,' she said now, 'if you could accept that Tim had only twenty-six years.'

Alix gave her a thoughtful, wary look. 'You're saying that if we had gone to Corfu that year it would have happened just the same? I wish I had your faith.'

'I'll pray that something might happen to clear the past away. You're a very pretty girl, Alix, and you won't have your youth again. These last two years have been abysmally wasted.'

'Wasted?' Alix smiled drily. 'I did get the business back on its feet.' Tim's father had died about the time they married and Tim had taken over, but under his extravagant direction Johnston's Plastics had gone steadily downhill. Tim had not been a dreamer, by any means, but he did seem to think one could dream money into the bank. After his death, Alix cleared out the extra assistants her husband took on, and from the grandiose office he built, she designed the plastics herself. Then she had gone out into the countryside in a functional van, selling

3

them. The original staff, left over from her father-in-law's day, recognizing that the honeymoon of Tim Johnston's reign was over and their jobs were at stake, had stood loyally by his very young widow and put everything they had into rejuvenating the business. Now, two years later, everyone had insisted she take a holiday.

'You'd be better to get clear of the business altogether and find a man to keep you,' said Lucilla now with conviction. She had had a very pleasant and quite useful life as the wife of the managing director of a steel organization and she reckoned these modern girls with their independent ideas were riding for, if not a fall, at least a pretty hard time. 'Perhaps it's just as well this old foot of mine is playing me up. Who knows who you might meet on a romantic Greek Island!'

Alix said with a shaky little laugh: 'If I had known from the beginning I was to end up going alone, I wouldn't have chosen Corfu.' The past was welling up all round her, even now. Suddenly, she had an almost uncontrollable desire to call the trip off.

Lucilla's shrewd eyes, as she watched her niece, were deeply concerned. It was her correct belief that Alix had still not by any means recovered from the death of that no-good husband of hers. She had plunged headlong into work with such intensity that it seemed now as though she may have

4

bypassed the open wound instead of living with it, drawing the edges together, and gradually mending them. Now, finding herself with time to brood for the first time since the funeral, it seemed as though she had discovered the wound still raw.

'Another coffee? No, not for me. What about you?'

'I'll just have a peep out and see how the queue is going.' Alix went to the door, saw the row of passengers had scarcely moved, and returned. Her eyes briefly met those of the man at the next table and she glanced away.

Lucilla tapped the folded newspaper she had laid on the table. 'There's nothing in here about Cary this morning. Perhaps they were going to drop him now.' Then speculatively, 'I wonder what Tim would have made of Cary's crash. He was plagued with envy of that wild cousin of his.'

Alix nodded. She thought Cary, the big business man, the successful, brash financier, had had a curiously paralysing effect on Tim. Tim wanted the money that seemed to come so effortlessly to his cousin, but he wanted it without trying.

'What an ass Cary turned out to be,' Lucilla commented.

'Fools may our scorn, not envy praise,
For envy is a kind of praise.'

5

'If they catch up with him he'll be taking a long look at a brick wall from the inside. You're well out of that whole thing, darling,' she said briskly. 'I am sure you'll see it one day.'

'When I get over feeling guilty about Tim's death.'

'You must forget that. You *must*.'

The cousins, Tim and Cary, had seen a good deal of each other during childhood for their parents had shared one of those Victorian houses that are too big and cumbersome to run alone in these servantless days. The two families had divided the house down the centre and shared the garden. Cary, five years older than Tim, was considered astute by the family though Alix's guardian, the outspoken Aunt Lucilla, had pronounced him on their first and only meeting as 'sharp.' In his early twenties, Cary, after making a good deal of money by gambling, went into finance and property. During the ten years when he had been on top of the heap Tim had seen less and less of him and consequently, Alix did not know him very well. They met once at her own wedding, once when Cary and Dora came to dinner, and again at a party Cary gave at their big house on Richmond Hill. He had drunk a lot that night and so, for that matter, had Dora. Alix remembered Dora standing on a table while Cary sang loudly:

6

'Sweet Lass of Richmond Hill.' The noise had wakened the child Benjamin who appeared sleepily, in pyjamas, in the doorway. Cary had insisted, at four o'clock in the morning, on teaching the boy to sing the song. 'For your mother,' he kept saying, 'my lass of Richmond Hill,' and Dora, prancing foolishly in her couture gown, had warbled: 'I'm the lass of Richmond Hill.'

Two years ago Tim, envious of his cousin's immense success, anxious to insinuate his way into Cary's glittering life, had wangled an invitation for himself and Alix to accompany them to Corfu. But: 'What do we do for money?' Alix had asked him. 'And clothes to keep up with Cary and Dora's rich friends?' It would not have been her kind of holiday, anyway, and though Tim would never have admitted it, she felt it was not his, either. How much better that they should see the island their way, with the eyes of Durrell and Lear, of Prospero and Ulysses. She could not see Cary and his jet-set friends leaving their luxury hotels to smell the scents of juniper and myrtle; to hear the sheep-bells, or pat the donkeys browsing beneath the olive trees. She had tried to tell Tim this, that more than money kept them apart from his cousin, but he only said: 'Cary knows how to live.'

'We would end up borrowing, and then what a pickle! Forget about Corfu. Come

7

with me to Yorkshire,' she had begged him. There lay the guilt. Tim sulkily agreed in the end, but reminding Alix that old ladies bored him: 'I'll drive up on Monday,' he said, 'when you have finished the chat with Lucilla.' On Monday there had been fog patches on the M1. Foggy death traps for a man who always drove at speed.

Lucilla's voice brought her back to the present with a rush. 'I wonder if you saw that article in one of the papers yesterday, I forget which one, about how easy it is to get false passports? Cary and Dora and the child could be in South America by now. You can get anywhere in a fortnight these days.'

'I dare say.' Alix knew why her aunt was gnawing at the same old bone. She had intended to take Alix to Corfu herself. She had literally forced the venue on her, and now she was more than disturbed at having to let her down. Alix knew the island well enough culturally, but had never visited it. 'It has become a bogey in your mind,' Lucilla had said, truthfully enough. Her husband had been a pilot in the last war. She knew all about getting back into a plane again after a crash. It was muddled thinking, in a way, that Alix should visit the place where she and Tim could have been when he was killed on an English motorway. On the other hand, there was a grain of sense in it, or would have been if she had gone there in Lucilla's

8

forceful company. Of course, these package trips were insured against disasters. Alix could have cancelled. But she had gone to a good deal of trouble to arrange for the smooth running of the business for this particular two weeks. It would cause too much of an upheaval if she changed the date. And she had no friends who could stop work and step in at such short notice. Besides, she considered herself to be a girl of character. Once she got through this initial day she was sure she would find herself capable of laying her own ghosts.

Alix glanced at her watch. 'Don't worry about me, Aunt. It's rest and sunshine I need and that will be there whether you go or not. It is very disappointing, but there ... life's full of tricks. I had better get along.' She helped Lucilla to her feet and they went back into the hall. The queue had melted away. She presented her ticket and saw her suitcase whisked off. She smiled faintly, apologetically, at the dark-haired, tall man she brushed against as she turned. 'Goodbye, Aunt. I still feel bad about dragging you all the way out here.'

'I had to go to the clinic, didn't I? And it made a pleasant detour.'

'Some detour.' They laughed together. 'Now, see you do go for the treatment—every day. Promise.'

'I promise, darling.' They kissed and Alix

went through to the Departure Lounge. Now that her aunt had gone she felt infinitely depressed. The plane was due to leave in fifteen minutes. She leaned against a pillar, waiting for the call, staring at the floor, oblivious to the bustle round her, oblivious to the man who had followed her in.

'Good God!' he said to himself suddenly. He pulled a wallet out of his pocket, slid a newspaper cutting into his palm and frowned at it. The picture was indistinct. A laughing face, with head thrown back. Short hair. He looked up at Alix. No, he said to himself with certainty. And thank goodness for that. The picture, now he came to look at it in comparison with real flesh and blood, could resemble half the girls in England. A typical—well, to be corny, English rose. It just went to show how tricky this assignment could prove.

Alix's thoughts were far away, on the strange coincidence that had brought Tim's disgraced cousin Cary Johnston into the news just at the moment when she was planning to go to Cary's favourite holiday resort, Corfu.

'Will the passengers for Flight 477 please go to gate 11.' Alix looked up, noted she had been standing by gate 11 and went through, still deep in thought.

\* \* \*

10

As the plane roared over the coastline leaving the English Channel far behind Alix did not notice the little old gentleman get up from the seat beside her and move off down the plane corridor, nor hear his exchange with the man who accosted him as he stretched his legs.

'Would you like a drink?' She turned from the window and looked up into the eyes of a smiling stewardess. 'Thank you. Vodka and tonic.'

'I'll have the same,' said the man beside her and involuntarily Alix glanced up and did a double take. Where had he come from? There had been a little old man with a hooked nose and spectacles sitting there before. She heard the young man say: 'That is for the two, and a double whisky for the gentleman in F14.'

'Please, no,' she protested, hastily opening her handbag, but the man paid and the trolley was moving off. 'How—?'

He broke in, eyes twinkling, voice innocent. 'The gentleman who was sitting next to you doesn't like being over the wing. The noise of the reverse thrust on landing frightens him. We swapped seats to save his nerves.'

She recognized him as the man who had been sitting close by in the lounge. 'Thank you for the drink.' She turned again to the window, faintly irritated by his nerve.

11

'Have you been to Corfu before?' he asked pleasantly.

Well, he had paid for the vodka. And he had the virtue of at least being original. She gave him a quick, appraising look. He had very alert blue eyes with dark lashes, a faintly Roman nose, soft, shiny dark hair that fell lightly across his forehead and turned in behind his ears, and when he spoke his mouth tilted at the sides, mischievously. 'I nearly went there,' she said in reply to his question, 'two years ago.'

'What happened?'

'I went to my aunt in Yorkshire instead.'

He smiled, half-puzzled, half-amused. 'Was that a better choice?'

'No. As a matter of fact, it was a disaster.'

'And so you're doing now what you should have done before?' He eyed her enquiringly.

'My aunt thought it might be a good idea—Corfu. Then she had to drop out at the last moment to have treatment for an old injury to her foot.'

He waited for her to go on explaining, but she had turned towards the window again. 'What can you see out there now?'

Alix started, blinked, realized she was looking blankly into a white foam of cloud and replied drily, laughing a little in spite of herself, 'Nothing at all.'

He said in an easy, conversational manner: 'You have chosen a good time. There are not

12

too many tourists in June and the weather is superb.'

'Is it? Good.'

She felt, rather than saw his eyes on her wedding ring. 'Are you going to join your husband?' he asked.

'My husband is dead.'

'Oh!' The lively opportunism fell away from his manner and inevitably a shocked, embarrassed silence drifted heavily around them. She wished she knew how to avoid it, or having made it, how to overcome it. In the event, a stewardess brought them back to the right plane. 'Here comes our plastic lunch,' Paul said.

'It's not so bad. I've a whole quarter of tomato, and that is beautifully preserved lettuce. Real, deep frozen, battery fed, guaranteed odourless chicken, too.'

Alix laughed. 'You travel frequently?'

'Frequently. But I don't often have such luck. I read once that if you get on immediately with a stranger it's because you were together before.'

'Before?' she repeated, puzzled.

'In another incarnation. On another planet. Or the spirit world.'

She found herself laughing again, mentally giving him top marks for style. 'Are you going to join friends?' She could not imagine a man of such charm and thrust being short of a holiday companion.

13

'No. My trip is really business.'

'What on earth sort of business does one do on Corfu?'

'Business is everywhere,' he rejoined carelessly and changed the subject. 'Where are you staying?'

'Paleocastritsa.'

'Ah!' he said knowledgeably. 'Paleocastritsa, the capital of King Alcinous of the Phaeacians.'

'It doesn't look like the capital of anything on the brochure which shows only a small taverna set among olives and a bay and a monastery.'

'The monastery of the Virgin Mary, the Panaghia, set high on a rock over the bay. You must take a stroll up there. The view is magnificent. Did you know the water is so clear you can read the print of a newspaper under water—that is, if you read Greek. Dive for them if you're a "Keep Corfu Tidy" sort of girl.'

'I am, so I may do that. You obviously know Paleocastritsa well.'

'I've read the guide books. If you're really strong of leg, there are the ruins of a 13th-century castle on the peak of a jagged mountain chain that ends way up behind the bay. It's a lovely island. Ulysses was said to have been washed up at Paleocastritsa. It's where he fell in love with the beautiful—' he stopped, his attention taken by a stewardess

14

in a very short skirt hurrying by.

'Nausicaa,' Alix supplied innocently. 'And Ariel cast spells amid broom groves and pole-clipt vineyard.'

It was his turn to do a double take. His eyes flickered, his mouth tilted, and he looked away. The plane's engines roared through the silence. A moment later he said softly: '*Touché!* Serves me right for showing off. Where are you staying?'

'At the Scheria. Do you know it?'

'Sabri's. Yes, I know it. Very Greek. You'll like it. And you'll find the staff very friendly.' He ran a critical eye down the length of her slim figure, reappraised her lack of make-up, her quaint hair cut, as unostentatious, as soft and smart as his own, her bulky charm bracelet and wide, studded leather belt. 'Sabri's is right for you,' he said, and she felt obscurely complimented, but faintly thrown.

She knew no more about him when they landed at the narrow strip by the Ionian Sea and she felt a pang of disappointment as he disappeared in a taxi with a jaunty wave and not even an exchange of names. Well, he was on business, and no doubt he was going to be kept fully entertained. For all she knew he might be returning to England tomorrow. A pity. Odd, that he should have contrived that quite audacious seat change if he never intended to see her again.

15

# CHAPTER TWO

She climbed aboard the taxi that had been provided as part of the package deal and ran through the new part of Corfu town. They swept along the waterfront heading away from the town and the high-rise flats and hotels, through a little Greek village with quaint narrow streets and plain little shops, then along the seashore and eventually into a dark green, hilly countryside that even in June was beginning to dry. Past market gardens and little fields of maize: a fat woman sitting side-saddle on a tiny donkey: past a clay road sloping up in the distance with a cloud of dust settling: then away from the glass-smooth water and into the cypress-clad hills where tiny orange groves nudged up against the road, the pink of the oleander brightened a wayside shrine, and the silver plumage of olive trees rose from twisted, age-old trunks.

Twenty minutes later they nosed round a bend in a cypress-wooded mountain and there was the sea stretched out into limitless miles beneath them. The road wound down in hairpin bends past a great luxury hotel and then another, dug into the rocky, unyielding ridges above an isthmus dotted prettily with olive trees, a basin where a large yacht lay at anchor and some picturesque villas clung precariously to a sloping cliff garden. Then they were hemmed in momentarily by high banks and bushes before bursting out into an idyllic cove where high cliffs rose on either side and that Panaghia monastery stared down at them, starkly white amid the deep green of the cypresses and against the sapphire blue of the sea. On the left was a white sickle of beach, a few stone pines and a brown taverna with coloured umbrellas laid out on what might pass here on this heat-ridden island for a lawn. To the right lay a low pink building on two floors with its restaurant sprawling out toward the road.

A squat Greek with hair as thick as a doormat and a used brown face leaped agilely down some stone steps, and opened the car door with a flourish. 'Missus Johnston! You are Missus Johnston? Yes, we are expecting you. I am Sabri. Welcome to Paleocastritsa.'

Holding the door open Sabri watched with admiration and a friendly smile while she descended, taking in with curiosity totally devoid of insolence her slimness, her white skin. 'Lovely day. The sun always shines here. All holiday.'

'That's super,' she smiled at him.

He manhandled her bag up the steps, then shouted at the top of his voice: 'Spiro!' From somewhere behind the building a slim, dark-eyed boy appeared at a run. Sabri spoke to him in Greek, then turned back to Alix. 'You have been here first time?' he asked quaintly.

'This is my first visit. Yes.' She smoothed her creased trousers and looked round appreciatively. The man on the plane had been right. She had chosen this place from a brochure, accidentally, but she had indeed chosen well. The hotel was long and low with a balcony running its full length upstairs. Here, through an open door she could see a bare kitchen, spotlessly clean, containing a scrubbed table and a large stove. The rest of the ground floor appeared to consist of a large pillared verandah set with tables and chairs, and shaded prettily with some sort of bamboo or cane.

'What a charming place!'

'Very nice,' agreed her host with satisfaction. 'Very nice bay. Good swim. Fish. Boats. The boy take you to your room. You have big balcony.'

'Thank you.' She glanced again at the tables, romantic with their floral offerings and saw herself, with a pang, sitting solitary at dinner.

'You want swim?'

'No, no. I will swim in the morning.'

'Okay.' He went back inside and Alix followed the boy up a narrow stone stairway. At the top there was an entrance door, then a long, empty corridor with half a dozen closed doors off it. He opened one of them and there was a bare little room with neat twin beds, a board floor, a small dressing table and through a glass door and across the big railed balcony a spectacular view of the bay with the two cliffs rearing up on either side.

'Bath!' said Spiro, smilingly opening a door in the corner and displaying a tiny bathroom with considerable pride.

'How lovely.' She fumbled with the catch of her bag.

'Okay,' said the boy cheerfully, and with a wide, good-natured grin, shot out of the door.

Alix opened the glass doors and wandered across the balcony. On her right the ragged coastline lay, cliff-rent, rock-strewn, green and silver leafed, hauntingly beautiful.

Far away behind her on the highest peak of the tree-studded mountain was the ruin of that 13th-century castle the stranger on the plane had mentioned. The Castle of the Angeloi, as Alix knew it to be, despots of Epirus. Looking round the rugged, wooded countryside with its dark green cypresses and silver olive trees, she said to herself with a curious mixture of relief and surprise: Tim would not have been at home here.

Why should Cary have loved Corfu? You can have the same party in any five-star hotel anywhere in the world, given the Martini set are there.

She looked out across the stretch of blue sea, its colour bleaching in the afternoon light, at the rearing cliffs behind, cypress-plumed and starkly grand against the sky. Perhaps, with the help of Aunt Lucilla's prayers, she was going to be able to clear with the past here, after all.

*     *     *

It was a beautiful beach, golden with sand, patched with sea-washed stones, and behind lay the olive grove, pale green and silver on the little strip of land between the bays. Alix lay stretched out in her bikini, paperback in hand, thinking she had never seen anything so peaceful or so lovely.

Further along, where the beach curved, a big red caique lay and now a stream of blond, well built men carrying scuba diving gear came hurrying across from a villa beyond the hotel, calling to each other in German. Alix watched them loading up the caique and then the engine burst into life and they chugged out towards the headland. No one had come here alone, except herself.

One of the men she had seen at breakfast approached: 'Hallo,' he said with a friendly smile, taking in her wet hair, her sand-caked limbs, 'you've already been in? What is the water like this morning?'

'The water is lovely. Fresh though. I wish I had brought snorkel and flippers.'

He dipped his mask in the sea, swirled a little water round the glass and shook it out again on to the sand. 'You're welcome to borrow these when I've had a go.'

'Oh, I didn't mean—'

'Don't worry. I am delighted to loan them.' He waded into the shallows and took off. He came back half an hour later and handed her his mask and snorkel. 'It's worthwhile going round by that point. There are some lovely fish among the rocks, and pretty marine flora. Do you swim well?'

'That's awfully kind of you. Yes, quite well.' He watched her as she swam fast, head down, looking through the goggles at the sea-life below.

His wife came across the beach to join him. 'Hallo, where is the gear?'

'Sorry, dear. I've just loaned it to that tall blonde. She doesn't look very happy and I noticed she's wearing a wedding ring.'

She took his arm affectionately. 'I brought you here to get you away from other people's problems.'

He gave her an apologetic smile. 'We might ask her to have lunch with us. She was here last night. I saw her sitting alone on the balcony. But she didn't turn up for dinner.'

They settled down on the beach and eventually Alix came in, swimming slowly and still looking down at the sea floor. She jumped erect in two feet of water, pulling the mask off, shaking out her wet hair. 'It's absolutely fabulous,' she called as she came up the sand. 'Thank you very much. I shall have to go into Corfu town and find some of these things. I've never seen such lovely coloured seaweed, and aren't the rock colours beautiful? Really,' she exclaimed ecstatically, 'it's another world!'

He took the proffered gear, smiling at her. 'Good. I'm glad it worked.'

'A friend—someone, told me you can read a newspaper on the sea floor. It's true. I found a bit stuck between two rocks, quite twelve feet down.'

'You read Greek?'

'No, no. But I could certainly make out the words.'

He said kindly: 'My wife and I were just going for a drink. Would you care to join us?'

'I would. Thank you very much.' He noted the quick acceptance, the thinly veiled gratitude, and was glad he had asked. They introduced themselves. He was Dr Brian Langley, and his wife, Jane.

'I am Alix Johnston.'

There was a plain little taverna directly behind them selling ice creams and coffee and drinks. They gathered up their things and put them into a little pile, then chose a table that was shielded from the sun by a

22

conical thatch.

'Are you on your own, or is—er—someone joining you?' Jane's eyes fell accidentally on Alix's wedding ring then slid guiltily away.

'I am on my own. Yes.' Alix assumed a carefully casual tone, looking up as she spoke at the purple blaze of bougainvillaea on the taverna wall behind them, trying to choose between the embarrassment of creating a mystery and the discomfort of sympathy.

'What will you drink? Jane and I have been trying ouzo.'

'That's the local tipple, isn't it? Yes, I'd like to try it.'

'If you're serious about acquiring the swimming gear,' said Langley, 'we can take you into Corfu. We've hired a car and it's due to be delivered tomorrow.'

'That's very nice of you. I would be grateful.'

'There is a little taverna half way up the road among trees. Jane and I thought we would go there for lunch today. Do come with us.'

'Oh, er, no, really—'

'Do you know anyone on the island?'

'No. No, I don't.'

'That's settled, then.' They both smiled at her and in friendly fashion raised their glasses. 'The Greek lunch starts about two. If you're ready then, it's only a few minutes' walk up the road.'

Alix went in to change about mid-day. The strength of the sun was a mild shock and she had no wish to burn. The shower in the little bathroom worked magnificently but owing to a whimsical quirk in the plumbing, the used water flooded up through a vent in the floor as it tried to run away. She stepped carefully over the small lake and dried herself in the bedroom, dressed in a very short sun dress, and slid her feet into sandals. Outside, some taxis had pulled up and a little group of Germans were ordering tables for lunch while the rest of the party made its way over to the beach. The boy Spiro was standing guard over a bucket containing a swirling, crawling collection of brownish claws and feelers that turned out, on closer inspection, to be live lobsters.

'You want lobster for lunch, Missus? You choose him?' Spiro looked up at her with eager black eyes, then reached gingerly into the water and drew out an angry brute with flicking tail and dangerous-looking claws. He held it up with pride. 'You like this one, Missus?'

'I'll choose one tomorrow,' Alix promised. 'They look super.'

'You don't eat? And no dinner last night?' Spiro was deeply concerned.

'Oh yes, indeed, I do eat very well. I was tired last night after the journey. And today I am going out with friends, but this evening I

24

shall certainly be here to dine. Tell me, where does that little path lead?' She pointed to a narrow track that ran away from the taverna and disappeared between two tall rocks.

'Into the olive grove. You can go to the next bay.'

'Is it a good place to swim?'

Spiro shrugged. 'Maybe. But it is better here.' He gestured across the road toward the beach where she had spent the morning. 'You go walking? Is nice.'

'Yes, I thought I would. I've time to fill in.'

On the opposite side of the road a man was engaged in a heated discussion with Sabri. He looked up and inexplicably her heart did a little flip. He was not smiling now and with the lightheartedness peeled away his face was hard, a little daunting. Then, as he recognized her that lively look transformed his features. He nodded, waved a hand briefly then turned his attention back to Sabri again. 'What is that girl's name? The tall one who came yesterday—in the blue dress.'

'Girl?' repeated Sabri critically. 'A very nice lady called Missus Johnston.'

'Johnston?' He asked sharply. 'That's the name of the man—'

'I don't know,' Sabri broke in. 'Not my affair. I am hotelier and restaurateur. You

25

have English troubles, you keep in England. Your politics nothing to do with us.'

The man grinned. 'Greeks! Can't you conceive of a crime that's not concerned with politics?'

Sabri sliced the air between them as though he would physically sever the thread of conversation. 'No, no. Always politics. And nothing to do with the lady Johnston. You show me photo. Is not her,' he pointed out with magisterial certainty. 'Perhaps name Johnston like Spiro in England,' he suggested, his black eyes bright, darting warning sparks. 'Everyone in England called Johnston, eh? Very common name?'

## CHAPTER THREE

Alix smiled, hesitated, wondering if he was going to come over and speak to her. But he was in earnest conversation with Sabri. Sabri's hands were going like windmills and she could see he was a little angry. She turned, not wanting to disappear without speaking to the man, and yet not wanting to seem to be hanging round. She took a few steps along the road towards the path she had intended following and suddenly he was striding across the intervening space, pushing something he had held in his hand

26

down into the breast pocket of a linen jacket he wore. 'Good morning, Mrs Johnston,' he called.

She turned. 'Good morning. You seem to have a certain advantage. I don't know your name.'

'Paul Crispin,' he replied. Those clear blue eyes were brilliant and they took in every inch of her. Short dress. Bare legs. Damp hair. 'I had to dash out here on business. How are you getting on? Everything up to expectation?'

'Great. Really great.'

'I thought you'd like it here. This area is the best. I see you've had a swim.'

'Oh yes. First thing. Someone loaned me a mask. You're right about reading under water. How extraordinarily clear it is! Where are you staying?'

'In Corfu. I'm not on holiday, you know. I only wish I was. I say, I'd like—' he broke off as a horn blared loudly behind him. 'That's a friend of mine who's in a desperate hurry. I'll have to go, but—' The horn blared again and he cast a look of intense exasperation in the direction of a taxi. It had turned round and was pointing back up the hill, with engine running. 'Damn! Put a Greek in a car and he goes berserk. Look, I've got to go.' He was already half way across the road, running backwards. 'I'll be back here about two thirty. Have lunch with me.'

'I can't.' She started towards him as he threw the words at her, half invitation, half demand. As he finished, the horn gave a final blast, drowning her refusal. The car had already begun to move slowly forward. She saw him leap in, heard the slam of the door, and then with a crashing of gears the car spurted forward and roared away up the hill.

Alix stood looking after it. Damn! What a pity she had accepted the Langleys' invitation! Lunch with Paul Crispin could have been fun.

Sabri came towards her across the road. 'You know him? Friend of yours?' His face wore a surprised expression.

'No. I talked to him on the plane, that's all.'

'So.' He shrugged his shoulders and disappeared into the hotel.

Alix looked at her watch. It was nearly half past twelve. An hour and a half to go before she had to meet the Langleys. She heaved an enormous sigh of sheer disappointment. By the time Paul returned she would be at the taverna in the trees. She could do no more than leave a message with Sabri.

Beyond the rocks the hill rose and there were narrow, rough steps to climb. She followed the winding track where it cut through between some dry, spiky bushes and came into the olive grove proper. Here the lovely gnarled trees grew in a casual sort of order along grassy terraces built up between stone walls. The ground began to slope away here and there was the rattle of a tiny stream over stones. She went and stood at the stream's edge, looking down into the narrow funnel of sparkling crystal water, diamond bright where it caught the edge of a rock and leaping into the air touched a ray of golden sunshine.

There was a wall ahead now. She hesitated a moment, then climbed over and found herself on a steep hillside. Here were ancient olives, the trunks so divided and twisted one could see through the gaps as through a Henry Moore sculpture. There were cypresses growing singly, prickly bushes, large boulders and patches of stones. She came across another tethered goat, chewing rapidly, holding his head high with surprise, his eyes alert but unafraid.

Feeling rather sad about the turn the day had taken, she moved on and came out suddenly in the open with the sea spread before her, leaden in the mid-day heat. For long moments she stood looking down at it, thinking of Tim, and Cary and Dora and the fact that she, the only one of the four of them who had not wanted to come to Corfu, was here. Odd, that it was so much her place, with its classical connotations, its unsophisticated air, its sense of peace. So little theirs. Maybe Lucilla was right, after

29

all, she thought and felt a faint stirring of gratitude. Maybe I had to come here. But not, surely, alone. A string of fishing caiques lay half way to the horizon, tiny as toys on the vast sea, and another one was on its way round the far point, towing five smaller caiques behind.

She shook herself out of her reverie. If she continued downward on this path, she should come out in the bay Spiro had mentioned and then there might be a track back round the rocks. There was a fringe of thick bushes just before Alix broke through to the sand, and then there was a small deserted cove with clear blue water and a jumble of rocks. Away above, on a pinnacle, lay what remained of the castle of the Angeloi, its white walls gleaming in the sun. In spite of the shade the olive trees had afforded her, Alix was very hot. She pulled her shoes off and stepped into the water. It was warm here. It must have been degrees warmer than in the cove. She cupped her hands and used them to splash her hot face. On the other side of the rocks a small boy had emerged and with back turned to her was paddling along the shore. He had blond hair like an English child, but surely no English child on holiday here would go down to the water dressed in a dark red shirt and blue jeans! Alix glanced at her watch, saw it was later than she had thought and went back to the dry patch of sand where her sandals lay.

The little boy was poking about with a stick now, bending down to pick up an object, absorbing himself in it. She saw then that he was eating something and guessed he had found hermit crabs in the sand, those bright pink creatures with strange, bare tails Dr Langley had described. He said one could get them out of their shells with a long pin and that the Corfiots relished them. She shuddered. He must be a local child, then. Alix turned and began to make her way back She was suddenly extremely hungry.

She crossed the beach and began to climb the rocks, then paused. The child was singing. She turned round, listening to the high sweet voice ... *I'd crowns resign* ... The rest was drowned by the swish and rustle of water round the rocks. Then it came again ... *call her mine* ...

Alix staggered, slipped and landed on her seat on a smooth rock, feet in a shallow pool. She stared across the stretch of golden sand at the little boy, thigh deep in the water, his back turned to her. I must have imagined it, she said to herself. An association of ideas out of her disturbed subconscious because she had been thinking of Cary and Dora. Because she had been thinking of Tim. But it came again ... *Sweet Lass of Richmond Hill*. There was absolutely no doubt about it.

31

That blond child over there, a child about the same size as Benjamin Johnston would be now, was singing the song Cary had taught his boy. But it could not be him! Cary, on the run from bankruptcy, scandal and the law, would not dare come here, to this island where he was known. And yet, heart hammering, she hurried forward. 'Benjamin!' she called uncertainly. 'Benjamin!'

His head came up and he swung round. He paused only long enough for her to see his face, pinched, piquant, and unfamiliar. Then he dropped his stick and dashed out of the water, splashing himself as he went, and pelted across the sand.

'Hi! Don't run off,' she shouted after him, but he was already gone, heading straight into the bushes from which she herself had recently emerged. 'Wait!' she shouted. 'Wait! Wait!' She fled after him, across the sand, across the coarse grass, then into the rough scrub that skirted the hill. There were several tracks running off here, all in different directions, and the boy was nowhere in sight. She called again. A Corfiot peasant boy, she said to herself feverishly, could sport fair hair, but would he have a light English-type skin? And why would he sing an English folk song?

*Sweet lass of Richmond Hill,*

Well, perhaps he was English. Why should he not know the song? Little Benjamin Johnston did not have exclusive rights to sing it. It might be that most of the children in England learned that song before they went to school. Cary and Dora would not hide here, on Corfu, for anyone might recognize them. Nonetheless, Alix started swiftly up the hill in pursuit. There was a frail, elfin look about that boy, a lonely air that had touched a chord of memory in her. She had seen Benjamin only that once, his pyjamas awry at four o'clock in the morning, his soft fair hair rumpled. How old would he be now? Five, six, perhaps? These thoughts raced through Alix's mind as she clambered up the steep and rocky path, dislodging stones, slipping and scraping her hands as she climbed higher.

The olive grove, when she reached it, was silent. If the boy was there, then he was hiding, and it would be easy enough to hide behind one of these gnarled, twisted trunks. Nevertheless, she felt he had gone. A child of that age was fleet of foot and could be half way to the village by now. Of course it was not Benjamin. I am too involved with the past, she said to herself. My imagination is going berserk. Aunt Lucilla was wrong to insist upon my coming here. She stood there for a while, waiting for her fast-beating heart to calm, waiting for the child to reappear, waiting with suspended disbelief.

Nothing happened. She turned and made her way back to the hotel.

## CHAPTER FOUR

The Langleys were waiting. Alix ran up to her room to change her sandals and collect some money. She passed Sabri standing by the kitchen door dressed elegantly in black trousers, a white jacket and bow tie. 'Sabri!'

'Yes, Missus Johnston. You have good walk?'

'Super, thanks. The gentleman who spoke to you, Mr Crispin, will be here shortly.'

'Okay. You go out? I tell him.'

'No. Tell him I have gone to the Taverna Calypso for lunch with Dr and Mrs Langley. Perhaps he might like to join us.' He looked at her with dark, thoughtful eyes, then patted her hand and turned away. Had he understood? But the Langleys were already moving off and she had to run after them.

The Taverna Calypso was set back off the road about a quarter of a mile up from the beach. It was a low, sand-colour building with a verandah. In front of it there was a half-circle of rockery and curved within its arc a concrete platform that could have been an open air dance floor, or band stand. Below again there was a big terrace set with tables. Some stood within the shade of trees whilst the majority, as at the taverna by the beach, had their own permanent conical thatch or a coloured umbrella.

'Let's sit here.' Brian drew out a light wooden chair for his wife and another for Alix, smiling at her. He liked pretty girls, but this one was more than that. She had intrigued him that first evening he had seen her sitting alone on the wide balcony they all shared. She had been deep in contemplative thought when he and Jane went down to dine and when they returned an hour and a half later she was still there, a blurred figure in the darkness. He had asked her to join them today because he felt she was reaching out for company. Now she seemed in some indefinable way beyond reach. And, oddly, disturbed.

'Let's start with an ouzo,' he said, speaking to a hovering waiter but including the women. 'Okay?'

'Fine.'

They scanned the English column on the menu. The waiter was quick with the ouzo but slow with the the soup. 'Nobody moves fast here,' said Brian. 'The Corfiots have a word for it. *Aurio*. Next year, sometime, never.'

'Like mañana?'

'Mañana plus.'

'That's good for you,' said his wife with satisfaction.

'It's good for all of us. What do you do for a living, Mrs—'

'Do call me Alix. My husband died, and I run a plastics business his father started.' The words fell easily from her lips. She could not understand how they had come like that, gracefully, so that there was no embarrassed silence. Was it the spellbinding tranquillity of this haunting island? Was that and only that enough to over-ride the past? Or was it the Langleys with their easy friendliness?

'You seem very young for both of those. To be a widow, and to be running a business.' Brian had a GP's aptness for putting tragedy in its place.

'I am really quite old. Twenty-four.' The Langleys laughed delightedly. 'And I worked for Tim's father before I met Tim. So when they both died, I was able to take over. I've been working for two years without a holiday, so they pushed me off to recover in the sun.' Explicit, sensible, unemotional facts. 'Ah! Here is the soup. Foolishly, I missed dinner last night. I could eat a horse.'

'You may have to. I am never inclined to order *bif-teck* east of the English Channel. But do try the moussaka. It's a splendid concoction that may owe its origins to the

36

occupation by the British, and cottage pie.'

'The British came here after defeating Napoleon, didn't they?'

Brian said: 'I've forgotten all the history I ever learned and I never mug up before going on holiday. Do you?'

'I've been interested in Corfu for some time. I had a rel—' she pulled up short, remembering the little boy, knowing he could not possibly be Benjamin, but remembering him all the same. 'My family came here,' she ended lamely. Then brightening: 'And I read Homer of course.'

They looked at her with respect and Langley repeated laconically, amusedly: 'Of course.'

'Cottage pie, indeed!' Alix said later, eating the lovely crusty layered cheese custard and eggplant and mince. 'If this dish does indeed owe its origins to the invading English, and I doubt that very much, English home cooking must have been a good deal more spicy and intriguing in Napoleon's day.'

It was nearly four o'clock when the waiter brought the local Koum Kouat liqueur and the tiny cups of over-sweet Greek coffee. The fact that Alix had been glancing surreptitiously at her wrist-watch every ten minutes since she sat down had not escaped Brian, and nor had the fact that she shot a frowning look from time to time back along the little path that led to the road. He was puzzled and faintly intrigued. He turned to his wife: 'Siesta, Jane?'

'Oh, isn't this dreadful? I've been stifling yawns. Well, why not? When in Rome...'

Alix said : 'I'll take a walk. And please, I must insist on paying my share of the bill.'

'You're our guest.'

'No, indeed. You were kind enough to give me your company. But—'

'No buts.' The doctor took the bill and rose. Alix rose too but Jane reached out a restraining hand saying: 'It's no use. Another time.'

Embarrassed, Alix turned half away and as she did so she jolted to attention. Perched on a tree stump near the back and to the right of the taverna, less than a hundred yards away, his thin legs drawn up under his chin, his face a blur in the shadow, sat the little blond boy she had seen on the beach. He was still wearing the same clothes, the red shirt, the old torn jeans. Brian was paying the waiter and as he pocketed the money and began to turn she asked: 'Who is that little boy? The little fair-haired boy sitting on the log?'

The waiter's eyes slid away, but his face was deadpan.

'Do you understand?'

'Probably not,' said her host equably. 'They only know restaurant English.'

But she was certain the waiter did

38

understand and did not wish to reply. 'Is the child a Corfiot?' she asked. 'He is very fair.'

The Langleys turned round to look. 'Lots of Corfiots look English,' Jane said. 'The English were here for fifty years!' She yawned. 'Well—'

'I'll leave you here,' Alix said, suddenly making up her mind. 'I'll take my walk up through those olive trees.'

'Right. See you later.' The waiter had walked away. She looked after him, eyes narrowed. He had gone to join two other waiters who were standing at the perimeter of the fast-emptying tables. Disconcerted, she saw they had moved into a little huddle and were darting suspicious glances at her.

She went towards the taverna. The path led up on the left hand side where a grocery store, closed for the siesta hours, jutted out, a little from the main structure. She climbed some stone steps and found herself behind the building. She went carefully down the narrow track between the back of the building and the yard. There was an open door from which came robust cooking smells. White-capped chefs stood at ease round a big centrally situated stove that was jammed with enormous pots and pans. Racks of plates stood round the walls. The hustle and bustle of lunch was over and they were packing away. One of them glanced up, saw Alix and smiled, a little surprised.

Suddenly there was a light scuffle of footsteps ahead and the boy she sought slipped out from behind a vine-hung doorway with a cooked chicken in one hand and a long bread roll in the other. He did not see Alix because he had turned in the opposite direction and was making a very hasty getaway. He leaped up the low bank, ran past the chicken pen, skirted the donkeys and disappeared into the shadow of the olive trees beyond.

So, one thing was settled. The child did not belong here. The son of the proprietor or a member of the staff would scarcely be purloining food. She would have one more try at placing him. She turned back towards the kitchen. One of the chefs had emerged and was watching her with friendly curiosity. 'Do you speak English?' He indicated that she come inside, then spoke in Greek to a kitchen hand. The man turned and looked at her. 'Yes. I spik Eeengleesh.'

'I saw a little boy with fair hair sitting on a tree trunk out there whilst I was having lunch. Can you tell me who he is?'

'One of the tourists, perhaps.' He spoke to the others in Greek and suddenly the friendly atmosphere had gone. They eyed her with closed stares.

Baffled, Alix turned away. There was a narrow, stony track leading up through the olive trees. Well, she could try to find him.

He had gone this way. She began to climb. The grove rose, tier upon tier, the terraces supported by drystone walls. The track meandered back and forth up a rough stairway made of stones, then along the terrace and up to the next one on rocks where the wall had given way. For nearly an hour she kept going, zig-zagging in the munificent shade of the olives, up and up the steep slope. There was no sight nor sound of the boy. Then suddenly the terraces and the last row of silver olives were behind her and her heart sank as she saw ahead a dry, steep, crumbling slope; a mini-cliff. She might have turned back but for the fact that the silence was suddenly rent by the grinding gears of a bus and the piercing shriek of a horn. Using the dry little bushes for hand-holds, Alix clambered up the slope, her feet slipping and slithering in the stony soil. She moved gingerly from dwarf heather to dry sage, bracing her feet against stones, stumbling breathlessly as they gave way, clawing with her hands until suddenly she heaved herself over a rocky rim and there it was, a sealed road edged with this rough dirt ridge in which grew huge rock roses, wild parsley and thistles.

Here the sun beat down relentlessly on the smooth surface and the road hurled the heat back to shimmer in the air. Alix paused to wipe her face with a handkerchief and scrubbed her dusty hands. The thin cotton dress was soaked against her back and her legs were shaking uncontrollably from the climb. To the right the road ran downhill, and to the left lay the beginnings of a village. She set out towards it.

★    ★    ★

There were tiny square houses painted in the harsh Greek greens, brown and mustard; a street well where a black-clad woman was washing clothes, and a little farther along a group of men playing cards at a small wooden table in the shade of an overhang, with chickens strutting stiff-leggedly around them. There were geranium bushes, shoulder high in tiny gardens, and in the street, orange and lemon trees. It was squalid, and it was beautiful. White-painted steps, brilliant in the sunlight, ran up to a house set above a low bank, and across them an old fig drooped, dust laden, picturesque. The shops had begun to open after the siesta and old men were putting up awnings. An ancient woman in the inevitable black, her hair hidden by a black cotton scarf, her feet encased in heavy boots, gave Alix a friendly, toothless grin. So, this was the end of the trail! The boy's home ground. He had a long way indeed to go down to Paleocastritsa to do his stealing.

Ahead, there was a look-out, a curve of stone wall with bench seats. There was no one there except a small boy selling postcards and a bearded priest in his long black robes with stove-pipe cap. Alix sat down thankfully, leaning back and resting an arm along the cool stones. A waiter came from the shop across the road and she ordered beer, hoping it would be cold. It was. She drank it thirstily, then, placing the empty glass on the tiny table the waiter had brought, she leaned back against the cool stonework, looking over the vast expanse of olive groves and rocks and cliffs and sea, marvelling that an island could be so hot and yet so green. Marvelling that the terraced hillsides managed to hold through to the long, hot summer time the rain that came down in such torrents in winter.

Suddenly her attention was arrested by childish voices. She turned sharply round. The little dark boy who sold the postcards had been joined by her quarry and the two of them were now in animated conversation no more than thirty feet away. She rose warily and as warily approached them. Seen at close quarters, the little blond boy was very grubby. His clothes were stained with sea-water, white-ringed where the salt had dried, and the blond hair was lank. They had their backs half-turned and so did not hear her silent footsteps. She went right up to them before she spoke. 'Hallo.' They both swung round. The fair child looked up at her with eyes as blue as an evening sea or sky and fringed with long, curling lashes. Tim's eyes. Cary's eyes.

Momentarily, Alix was incoherent with shock. Then she managed: 'Benjamin?'

He looked at her warily, making no attempt to reply, nor yet to run away, and she looked back at him, the past flooding round her, the sheer magnitude of his presence taking her breath away. 'Benjamin?' Still he did not answer. 'Why won't you talk to me?' Alix asked. She reached out a gentle hand, touching the boy's shoulder. She could feel the little bones through the grubby cotton shirt. Still he stared at her unblinking. 'Where do you live?' she asked and when he still did not reply added: 'What are you doing here?'

His Greek friend looked shocked. 'Mustn't ask,' he said.

'Why not?'

'You mustn't ask,' he repeated. The fair boy took the opportunity to walk away. He went over to the store and stared in the window.

'What is wrong?' Alix asked the Greek boy. 'Why must I not ask about your friend?' When he made no move to reply she asked: 'Is his name Benjamin?'

'No. Spiro,' replied the boy.

'Spiro?' He nodded.

But could she be mistaken? 'Spiro who?' she asked supiciously.

At that moment St. Spiridon, the Corfiot benevolence, must have been watching over the children because a horn shattered the mountain peace and a little old bus rumbled up the narrow street to stop at the look-out. As the tourists began to descend, the Greek child moved forward, holding out his coloured postcards enticingly. The fair-haired boy who could be, must be Benjamin, came out of the shop, passed behind the bus, then without a backward glance set off towards the hills.

Alix followed him. At the corner he seemed to hear her footsteps and turned. A fleeting expression of panic crossed his small face and he began to run. Alix ran, too. Less than fifty yards apart, they rounded a bend and sped along a narrow stony road, around another bend, then along a flat stretch of perhaps a hundred yards that led over a hill. The heat was dreadful. The boy began to slow. He looked apprehensively behind, then started to run again. Alix was gaining on him now, and at the next rise where the road grew narrower and olives and cypresses began closing in, she caught him up. 'Look here,' she began coaxingly between gasps for breath, 'why do you run away from me? Why can't we be friends?'

He looked up at her, panting. His little face was drawn with distress. She put a hand on his arm, leading him over to the shade of a young olive and said very gently: 'My name is Alix. What is yours?'

He drew a long breath, half-gasp, half-sigh. 'S-Spiro,' he said in a very precisely English voice. 'S-S-Spiro.' He shook himself free of her hand and moved ahead again.

But he was not Spiro. He was Benjamin Johnston. There was absolutely no doubt in Alix's mind now. 'How old are you?' she asked.

'Five and a half.'

Yes, that would be right. She remembered Dora leaving the house in a hurry after Tim's funeral to pick up her little boy who had just started kindergarten. Benjamin would be under six still. 'What are you doing here, Spiro?' she asked.

He forged mutely on. She tried again. 'Who do you live with? Your father? Are your mother and father here?' A low-branched fig tree hung across the track with figs bursting pinkly through the black skins. She reached up and picked one, handing it to the child. He accepted it in silence, enclosing it tightly in his small fist. 'Don't you like figs?'

He looked down shyly at his feet in their worn and dusty shoes and began to kick

46

small stones along the track. 'Not much.'

'Are your mother and father English?' she asked warily. He did not reply and she tried again. 'Does your father work on the island?'

Still the boy did not answer. The road was narrowing down here to a mere rough track. There was a small plop as a fig dropped into the dust. Benjamin wiped his hand surreptitiously on his grubby trousers. There was a small dwelling of sorts on the right, here, with a whimsical scarlet door and the palings dark blue on the broken fence that ran along the front. Behind, a tiny lemon grove. An ageing fig tree hung over the gate which was held closed by an iron bar. They turned a corner then and came across an old woman following a little flock of goats. She wore black stockings, a long black gathered dress, and that now familiar white cloth wrapped loosely round her head like a strange hat. She looked very old, very weather-beaten. She smiled at Alix out of a toothless face dried like a brown prune. Then she spoke to the boy in Greek. He looked at her shyly and replied, also in Greek.

'You know all the people,' Alix ventured.

He nodded, then stared back at the ground again. 'Why are you coming with me?' His voice was uneasy.

'I wanted the walk. I've nothing else to do, and you looked a nice, friendly boy.'

47

'Do you want to see my father?'

'Well, yes. Is that all right?'

He flushed, but did not answer. At that moment they came to a rough and very primitive dwelling of sorts. Clustered together by the fence there was quaking grass, and thistle and old man's beard.

There was no gate, only some roughly hewn steps leading up to a wooden front door. The garish Greek paintwork was missing. What had been there had long since faded. Some fig trees growing in the starved, cement-hard garden, clawed at each other for support. The brooding hills around were silent. From overhead came the chattering of a jay perched in the branches of a Judas tree.

'Do you live here?' Alix stared at the hovel in mindless silence.

The boy nodded uneasily, sensing her shock. Alix stood in the track watching him as he went up to the front door. Suddenly, with a feeling of real apprehension, she wondered why she had come, and what she was going to do now. The door was slightly ajar. The boy pushed it open. Immediately a harsh male voice broke through the jay's metallic chatter. 'So you've come back, you little devil! What harm have you done, heh? Where have you been?'

The door swung wide and Alix could see the child cowering away across the bare room. 'Where have you been? Tell me that!

48

You've been in the sea, for one thing. My God! Didn't I tell you you weren't to go down there? Didn't I tell you?'

Alix's hand gripped the gate post. Was that Cary's voice? She could not tell. And even if it was Cary, she thought as apprehension flooded through her, was his presence here any of her business? Dora would be here, too. Part of her wanted to turn and run, but there was another part that held her feet in check. *Where was Dora?*

'Jesus!' The word came as an angry bark. 'Sweet Jesus! You went down there!' And then she saw a tall figure cross the room, heard a resounding slap of flesh on flesh and the child's terrified cry.


# CHAPTER FIVE

She did not remember afterwards dashing through the gate, only that she found herself in the doorway, looking in. The child was cowering in a corner and Cary had swung round, a gaunt, unshaven, wild-eyed Cary who was staring at her, his face livid with anger. The anger changed rapidly to shock and then to fear.

'What the devil are you doing here?'

Ignoring his question, Alix fled across the room. She picked up the cowering boy in her arms. He burst into tears and she gentled him against her shoulder. 'You got him into this,' she said acidly. 'Don't take it out on him.' She looked round for somewhere to sit. There was a wood-framed couch with a thin, lumpy cushion. She sat down on it, holding the child close. He sobbed noisily against her neck, great wet sobs with the tears splashing against her skin. 'Where's Dora?' she asked sharply.

Cary looked down at her, his face working, then swung round to the door and stood there a moment, looking warily out.

'It's all right,' she said cuttingly. 'I came alone. Where is Dora?'

He turned back to her. Those blue eyes that were so like Tim's watched her suspiciously. But the face bore no resemblance. Tim had a sort of asceticism, a touch of weakness. Cary's etched confidence of the past had now turned granite hard. The well-cut mouth was set, and a line ran deeply etched from nose to chin making him look ten years older than when she saw him last. But if his outer self was brutal, there was real fear fluttering behind his eyes. He ran a hand shakenly through his thick dark hair. 'Don't you know?' he asked, then added weakly: 'I thought, naturally, you would have been in touch.'

'I spoke to her on the phone several times, as you no doubt know. But she disappeared with you—so the papers said.'

She watched him closely, trying to read whatever it was had replaced the fear behind his eyes. Doubt perhaps? Suspicion? For a moment or two there was only the sound of soft, muffled sobs from the child.

He turned away, seated himself on a hard chair and said: 'I thought when I saw you you must have brought a message from her.'

She did not believe him. Expecting a messenger, he would not have looked shocked and angry like that. 'Why did Benjamin not stay with her?'

'It's how we planned it. Dora has work to do. She wouldn't have time to spare for him, and we thought he should have one parent.'

'What work? Dora has disappeared.' Watching him closely she thought she saw a flicker of relief in his eyes, then he said: 'That's good. The plan has worked—so far.'

'What do you mean? What plan?'

'Listen,' he said wearily, 'and I'll tell you. You know they were going to throw me into jail—'

'No, Cary. Not that! Surely you would have been remanded on bail!'

He gave a sort of thin sneer. 'May-be.' He pronounced the word slowly, sarcastically. 'But you don't know, do you? And once you're in court it's too late to get away. They don't send you home to pack a bag, you know. It's straight from the dock to the cells.

51

I could have cleared myself, given time, but they wouldn't give it to me. So we decided I would hotfoot it out of the country with the boy, and Dora would set about gathering up the facts.'

She felt a sense of relief. 'Then you would go back and—'

'Present the facts before an enquiry. On my terms.' He thrust out that dark, stubbled chin. 'Why should I lie around in jail while the slow wheels of the law turn? And they are slow, Alix, believe me.'

She could not understand how Dora could be making enquiries without the newshawks spotting her. 'Why do the papers say she has disappeared?'

'I have a good many rich and influential friends, you know that,' he replied obliquely. 'And in a red wig and cheap out-of-date clothes, believe me her own mother wouldn't recognize Dora.'

Benjamin was sitting up on Alix's knee now, looking at her with those compelling blue eyes. 'I don't understand why you've come here where you are known,' she said.

'Because I speak Greek, and because no one will give me away. Of course all the locals know about me. But the Greeks are nothing if not loyal and they like the English. Besides, they think I'm in political trouble. That's the natural assumption here and I haven't disillusioned them. All the same, the boy had no right to go down there. I've forbidden him to go past the village. And this morning he went to the beach. Look at his clothes! *That's* where he could be recognized—or forget himself sufficiently to tell English tourists his name.'

And it was not the first time he had been to the beach, Alix knew. Some local child had taught him to catch and eat hermit crabs. 'Let me take him to my hotel.'

'That's impossible.'

'Why? He has the same name. No one would question him with me there. If he plays up at the look-out where I found him he does have a chance of exposing you.'

'No. He knows he is not supposed to go to the look-out.'

'Cary,' she said beseechingly, 'you cannot keep a child here like this. A prisoner.'

'I'm his father, am I not? I can do what I like with him.'

Momentarily, she was shaken by the arrogance in Cary but compassion overcame it. 'He said his name was Spiro. Why?'

'It's a guard of sorts. A confusion. Call "Spiro!" into a crowd on this island and seventy per cent of the men and boys turn round. If there is someone on the look out for me I don't want some kid shouting "Benjamin!" at the wrong moment.'

'Of course. But Cary, he is only a little boy. He must be properly cared for. Properly

53

fed. He's as thin as a starved lamb.'

'Nonsense,' said Cary brusquely. 'He gets enough to eat. Don't you, Ben? Are you hungry?'

The child looked at Alix beseechingly. She glanced round the bare little room, wondering what had happened to the chicken. There was a small table, some wooden chairs. An empty shelf. One uncurtained window. A piece of sacking that was evidently used as a curtain, hung from one of its corners by a nail.

'Are you hungry, boy?' Cary's voice was a rough challenge.

'Not now.'

And that would be true, Alix thought sardonically. If he had taken proper advantage of that spitted chicken and bread roll Benjamin must be bursting at the seams. 'How do you get your food?' she asked Cary.

'A woman brings it down from the village. It's not always Benjamin's cup of tea, admittedly, but he'll have to get used to it. He always had plain food at home.'

'He is pathetically thin.'

'Nonsense. He was always a boney child.' Benjamin was poignantly silent, gazing up at her. She had to get him out of here. 'Let me clean up a bit,' she said briskly. 'Where do you keep a broom?'

He nodded towards a door on the right and she went in. There was a shallow stone

54

sink, a stove and an open door leading into a wilderness of garden. Stones, hard-packed earth, the ubiquitous fig tree, a little patch of corn wildly sown by a careless wind.

The back of the dwelling looked upon some shaggy hillocks that tumbled prettily out of a belt of cypress trees. Somewhere there must have been a wild rose for the scent lay dreaming on the air. She took a broom from its place against the wall, for there were no cupboards, and swept the floor. Cary was hovering in the doorway, looking a little irritated, watching her. Benjamin, who had still not uttered a word, disappeared outside. There was another door at the back of the living-room. 'What's in there?'

'That's a bedroom.'

She found a tiny room with two hard-looking, narrow beds, unmade, and a small window covered by a torn blanket. There was a badly marked mirror on the wall, a chest of drawers and one suitcase. There was a brashly coloured magazine cut-out of an icon on the wall, all gold and red, and above the bed a crucifix. She looked up to see Cary watching her. 'This is good of you,' he said gruffly. 'I don't know what to say.'

She paused in her work, leaning on the broom. 'I'd like you to say something about Benjamin.' She saw his mouth tighten and her heart sank. 'Look here, Cary, I don't know what you've done and I don't care very much. It's no affair of mine. But a child is everyone's responsibility.'

'He's being treated properly. And it won't be for much longer.'

'How long?'

'I—don't know yet.'

'And how will you find out, for heaven's sake? How will Dora get a message to you here?'

'I shall have contacts, later.' His eyes slid away.

She looked up at him with a sort of despair. 'Would you be willing to tell me exactly what happened?'

He brushed her question aside. 'It's too complicated. You wouldn't understand.'

She watched him. He was as jumpy as a cricket. 'I have been running Johnston's Plastics for two years. I'm not a bird brain.'

'Of course not. I didn't mean to insinuate that. But I doubt if you know anything much about the complexities of high finance. I've been dealing in millions, Alix. Some of it was concerned with government Ministers and government loans. And foreign money was involved. It all started to go wrong when the Arabs let us down on a deal because Israel was hotting up for an attack on the left bank of the Jordan. They blamed the British for being pro-Israeli and coolly cancelled a deal that had repercussions right down a long line. Some of the chaps who had put up money scarpered and I was left holding the bag. But it can all be explained, and maybe even put right if I can stay out of civilization long enough for Dora to assemble all the facts.'

Dora, trotting around England in a red wig pretending she was not his wife? It didn't make sense. He saw the doubt in her eyes, knew he had not put his case well enough, and said angrily: 'You don't begin to know what goes on. I've never read a thriller that could touch some of the real stories I've been concerned with.'

She straightened and began sweeping again. The dust was thick everywhere. He could not have done anything towards keeping the place clean. 'I'll do what I can to help you,' she said. 'And when I return I'll go and see Dora. But in the meantime you had better think about allowing me to take Benjamin with me. I think you've met my Aunt Lucilla. She would gladly move in with me and help look after him. He isn't happy here, and you're not caring for him properly. Whatever you say, the child looks—well, not ill, but certainly undernourished. And he ought to be at school.'

Cary had switched off. She could see it in the purposeful way he crossed the room and bent over the suitcase. 'There is something you could do for me,' he said, straightening. 'Would you go into Corfu town and pick up some mail?'

'Of course.' She brushed the dust into a little pile and leaned the broom against the wall.

'I'll have to give you my passport.' He was drawing something out of a pocket. He handed it to her. 'And for God's sake don't lose this.'

She flushed. 'Of course I won't lose it. But aren't you taking a chance, having mail sent here?'

'The passport isn't in my name.'

He watched the sudden shock in her face ebb away to give place to something like fear. She had not liked him having the child, but this was quite different. He had never known much about Tim's wife but he guessed she was built on Girl Guide lines. There was that extraordinary affair of her taking over Johnston's Plastics when it was going bust. For Uncle Charles's sake, she said. And him cold in his grave. What did she think Charles was going to do? Come back and haunt her if she didn't clean up the mess Tim left behind and get the firm going again? He had a momentary twinge of nervousness as he handed the passport over. He put a hand on her shoulder and looked down into her face. Yes, she was okay. Those clear eyes, the habitually serene face that smoothed out

58

quickly when the shock and fright subsided. He bent down and kissed her hard on the mouth. She drew back affronted, holding her fingers to her lips, her eyes rounded with a new kind of shock.

'Sorry,' he said. 'I should have shaved,' and when her eyes told him it was not that, he added brashly: 'Good God, girl, Tim's been dead two years. You've got to start again. We're both lonely, aren't we?' He grasped both her hands. 'I'd never realized—you're a beauty, aren't you?'

She pulled, but his hands were hard as iron. She relaxed because she knew she could never get away until he chose to allow it. And she was vulnerable, it was true, especially with Tim's eyes looking down at her. He kissed her again and this time she scarcely resisted.

There was a faint sound from the doorway and she swung round. Benjamin was eyeing them with a puzzled expression. 'You're always in the wrong place, aren't you!' muttered Cary.

Alix went over to the little boy. Her heart was hammering. She bent down and took his hand. She saw there was grease round his mouth and crumbs on his lips. She took a paper tissue from her pocket and surreptitiously wiped the tell-tale marks away. 'What do you do with yourself here, Benjamin?'

'Nothing.' She turned back to Cary, a protest on her lips, but before the words were out he said shortly: 'Don't make it any harder. This is something I cannot do anything about for the moment.'

'But you can. You can. Please let me take—'

'*No!*' The explosive answer silenced her. Holding the child's hand she led him across the mean little living-room and stood with him in the doorway. The sun was going down beyond the forested hilltop, and a pink glow touched with gold was spreading across the sky.

'You would be safer with Benjamin in my care,' she said. She did not want to tell him the boy had been not only to the beach but in full view of anyone who liked to dine at the Calypso, since the fairly obvious question of how she found him seemed to have by-passed Cary at least for the moment. She sat down on the doorstep and patted her knee. Benjamin's eyes were wary. 'Come on. You're not such a big boy!' He edged across and sat down. 'Have you got anything to play with?'

'No.'

'Any books?'

Benjamin shook his head. 'He is learning Greek from the locals,' Cary said brusquely. She ignored that.

'No toys?'

'No.'

Anger, frustration, bewilderment warred in her, and over them a profound and desperate pity for this waif caught up in the mess of his parents' life. Pity for Cary, too, for he was possibly numbed by his circumstances and rendered negligent and harsh by his living fear of day-to-day exposure. She said to Benjamin: 'I could go into the town and buy you some comics and toys. You'd like that, wouldn't you?'

The blue eyes lit up with excitement. 'Oh yes, please.'

'Right, I'll do that first thing in the morning.'

Cary disappeared into the bedroom. She whispered: 'Where is the chicken?' A flash of fear crossed the boy's face. 'I won't tell. But you mustn't do it again. Where is it?'

'In the garden.'

'You mustn't leave it there because it will gather ants and go bad. Promise me you will throw it away and I'll bring you another one tomorrow.'

The little boy nodded, big-eyed with gratitude. Cary came up behind them. 'It's very good of you. And while you're at it, do you think you could bring something Ben might like? Cornflakes, and a milk pudding or something of that kind. You might be able to get it in a tin.'

'Of course.'

61

'You're right, he hasn't been eating properly,' Cary admitted. 'Madame Vassilakis up in the village has been very good but she's got a heavy hand with the sort of stuff Benjamin is not accustomed to. Spices and peppers and such.' So, he was not so much insensitive to the child's well being, as thin-skinned with his own worries.

When it came to her leaving he would not allow Benjamin to walk alone with her up the road. He came too, with the boy between them, holding hands. He stopped where the track widened and kissed her again, lightly this time, for the benefit of a wondering child. 'Sorry about this,' he said ruefully, fingering his stubbly chin. 'Of course I have to grow a beard. I'll be a bit more free, with that for camouflage.'

She left them there and walked to the look-out, wondering whether she would brave the steep hillside with darkness descending or whether it might be wiser, and safer too, to use the longer, winding road. She decided on the latter. She wouldn't be much use to little Benjamin with a broken leg. Now that she was away from Cary's throbbing masculinity her mind cleared of emotion and she thought suspiciously: How could he have left in such a hurry! There had been time to get a false passport. It surely followed there must have been time to pick up a few books and toys.

# CHAPTER SIX

Miraculously, there was a bus grinding up the hill. Alix stood at the look-out while it deposited its half-dozen passengers and turned round. The sun had gone down dragging the colour out of the sea, leaving a motionless silver desert darkening to grey with hints of black. A curved line of fishing caiques, slung together like a child's train, frail with distance, lost form and smudged into the night. The birds in the trees above her head were already sleeping. Paleocastritsa, far below, lost its twin headlands and curled in upon itself for the night.

The bus was old, dusty and nerve-wrackingly noisy in the essential low gear. A peasant woman sat in the front seat carrying on a high-pitched conversation with the driver while the chickens in a box on her knee clucked irritably. The hill descended in a series of hairpin bends that were not in themselves hazardous but the driver, illustrating his arguments with eloquent hand-waving, was a threat.

She descended at the beach with a sigh of relief and was making for the steps at the side of the hotel when a lazy, familiar voice arrested her. 'That must be the longest lunch on record.'

She swung round. Paul Crispin rose from a small table shaded by an overhang of vine. 'Won't you join me?'

'I really am most terribly sorry.'

'I know. You forgot.' He spoke drily, but without rancour.

'No, no. Didn't Sabri give you my message?' He shook his head. 'I tried to tell you, but the horn was blaring and you were running away. I had already accepted an invitation to lunch.'

'I thought you didn't know anyone on Corfu.'

'Yes. I mean no, I don't.' Idiotically, she thought of Cary and her cheeks flared. 'We met on the beach this morning. I wonder why Sabri didn't tell you?'

'I wonder,' he reiterated.

'Don't tell me you have been waiting all afternoon for me!'

'I fitted in a swim and a very late bit of food. Scarcely lunch. Even the despairing need sustenance.'

'No, really, it wasn't as bad as that.' She liked the way he made her laugh so easily. 'Please stay and have dinner with me.'

'Would you like that?'

'I really would.'

'Let's drink to it, then. What will you have?'

'I like ouzo. Here's a waiter. His name, I

64

think, is Nico.'

Paul gave the order then settled back in his chair, looking at her. 'And where have you been?'

'Since lunch?' Playing for time, she asked the silly question mechanically.

He said drily: 'During lunch, you ate.'

'What super food!'

'Enjoy it while you can. There are only about half a dozen Greek dishes in these tavernas. You can get tired of them. So...?' He raised one eyebrow.

'My friends returned here for a siesta and I went for a walk.'

'Some walk.' Tiny coloured lights leaped into the vine above their heads and all through the restaurant behind. Paul squinted ostentatiously at his watch.

'Yes, it was some walk. Or rather some climb.' Nico came with the drinks and she watched them cloud up as Paul poured the water in.

'So, where did you walk?'

'Up that vast hill behind here. I came to a look-out in the end. It was a jolly long way.'

'You must have taken it mighty slowly if you went only as far as the look-out at Lakones.'

She affected vagueness, staring into her glass. 'I suppose I did. It was hot and I'd had a good lunch. The olives make excellent back rests.'

'Mmm.'

'Don't watch me like that,' she found herself saying nervously, then added with a quick smile: 'I must be a mess.'

'I'm sure you're not, although I can't see you too well by this one-watt bulb. I think you're lovely.' He watched her deliberately to see if she would flush, and she did. He liked that. It gave him direction. He had been perturbed about that business of the dead husband. But two years was a hell of a long time at her age. She could not be more than twenty-three or-four.

'I must go and shower and change. Oh dear, and you have already spent the afternoon waiting for me!'

He nodded, watching her still, intrigued that she should be so flustered. 'And there you are, going off again.'

'I'll tell you what. There's a big communal balcony outside the bedrooms, and some canvas chairs. Would you like to bring your drink up there? It's really wonderful at night, looking down on the water and across at the lights of the little taverna under the monastery hill. I'll be as quick as I can.'

'Right. I'll meet you there. I'll bring another couple of drinks.' He looked up and called: 'Nico!'

'No. I'll wait. The only access is through the rooms so I shall have to lead you. I don't suppose Sabri will mind.'

66

He grinned. 'Sabri isn't here to see. And by the way, the local band is coming here tonight, I'm told. That means Greek dancing with everyone invited to join in. Sabri leads. He calls himself the Pro-fess-eur of dancing. So, if you've a—' he gave her a droll look '—folk dancing dress, wear it. People turn up from villas and the other hotels.'

'Greek dancing! We-ll!'

She had brought several long cotton dresses for evening, flouncy and pretty.

'Thanks for the tip. I've never seen Greek dancing but I'm willing to try. Here's Nico with the drinks. Follow me. I hope he doesn't think I'm taking you in for what they call in the papers "immoral purposes".'

He grinned. 'As a matron, by Greek reasoning you can't be defiled. Virginity is the great thing, here. Once that's gone, the elders of the family stand round a widow with guns and iron bars. I should think by coming here unchaperoned you've already shot your bolt so I shouldn't worry.'

She laughed, but she gave him a sharp, suspicious look. 'Don't they have a different set of rules for tourists?'

He went through the bedroom and out on to the balcony carrying the glasses in his hands. As he passed the twin beds he gave her a lazy look from beneath his lashes. 'I wouldn't be surprised.'

She left him leaning on the rail and drew

67

the heavy woven curtains across her glass door. The passport with Cary's photo and the name Fuller she hid carefully in a drawer. Dressing swiftly, she heard voices outside. The doors were open and Paul's voice drifted across and through the curtain. 'No. I haven't moved in. I'm a friend of Mrs Johnston,' and Langley's surprised: 'Oh! I understood—' Then lamely: 'Jolly good.'

Alix sighed sharply, remembering she had told the Langleys she knew no one here. Life was always like that. She wished Paul had said they met on the plane. By the time she was dressed, Brian had returned to his room. She glanced briefly into the big mirror behind the wardrobe door. The gown was pretty with its double rows of flounces, and it suited her. The sun today had brought the blood to her skin and the warm pink glow enhanced the light tan she had picked up. She stepped out on to the balcony and Paul wolf-whistled her.

They stayed there for an hour, night-bound in this fairy-tale setting. The tables were nearly all full when they went down. Nico found them one close against the outer vine. The Langleys were seated near by. They gave her a queer look so she paused to introduce Paul. 'We met on the plane yesterday.'

She felt at ease then. 'Tell me what you're here for?' she asked Paul as they sat down.

68

'To see people. To look around.'

'Property developing?'

'No. There is to be no development in this area. Queen Frederika used her influence to see it remained natural.'

'The Queen hasn't much influence now.'

'No. But one hopes people will stay on the path she laid down. Enough resorts have been ruined. It would be sacrilege to spoil this.'

She noticed that he had discreetly moved the interest from himself to the bay and thinking inevitably of Cary, wondered if he, too, was up to some monkey business.

'Greek wine? I've no doubt Sabri would provide the French, but—'

'Oh no, no, no. The local plonk, please.'

Jane, watching them surreptitiously from the next table, said to her husband: 'That's nice, isn't it?'

'Yes, indeed. Looks like we can stop worrying about her, now.'

Afterwards, the waiters removed the tables from the centre of the floor and a small Greek band dressed in black with white frilled shirts and carrying violins and accordians, walked in out of the darkness. The Langleys' table was pushed up against theirs to expose a circle of tiles for the dancing. Paul insisted upon buying them a Koum Kouat. Then Sabri came in, eyes shining in his nut-brown face, one glorious gold tooth flashing through his smile, hands held aloft with elbows bent, fingers snapping. 'I will geeve you exhibition local dancing,' he announced. 'Very queek exhibition. Then, when you have watch, you join in. Is easy. And nice. Re-a-dy!' He caught Alix's eyes. 'Two minutes,' he announced, 'and I will take the prettiest lady and lead the rest of you. Watch!'

'That's you, darling,' said Paul good-humouredly, and the Langleys gave her an approving glance.

Alix sat up straight, cheeks flushed. 'Then I had better attend closely. I'd hate to lead you all astray.'

Paul watched her intent profile, marvelling a little at the change in her. Yesterday she had been asleep, passive, even sad. Now she was a-throb, not with excitement or even pleasure, but it was as though a pulse had been generated inside her where there had been stillness before. He had liked the way she had accepted, with a total lack of coyness, their assumption that Sabri had chosen her as the prettiest one.

The steps were simple enough for a novice to follow. Sabri glided between the tables. 'Missus Johnston.' Warmed by the good food and wine, the onlookers turned smilingly and someone clapped softly as the tall, fair English girl took the floor with the squat and sinewy little Greek.

'Johnston,' muttered Paul softly. Langley glanced at his intent face, wondering if he was talking to himself. Paul's eyes flickered up, questioning.

'I wondered,' Brian replied. 'We both wondered. You mean the financier, don't you?'

'Crossed my mind.'

'We-ll, it's a very common name.'

'His wife is fair.'

'Most English girls are,' put in Jane. 'I saw those pictures of Dora Johnston in the paper, but really you could liken her to a million English girls. It was the widow story that made me think. She's so young.'

Alix had not been casual when Paul drew the facts from her in the plane.

'The papers made much of their sojourns in Corfu. It did occur to us—After all, the police aren't looking for her. But where is the child?'

Jane said: 'Why would she come here? As a sort of—decoy?'

They dragged their attention away from the couple dancing and their eyes met accidentally, a little furtively. Brian was remembering that he had offered Alix a ride into Corfu town tomorrow. It would be interesting to see whether she did, in fact, know her way round a town she professed not to have visited. Still, it was none of his business and he had no intention of getting

71

involved.

He would have been surprised if he had been at the big hotel up the hill later that evening when Paul's hired car pulled up outside. He went in and asked the night porter if he could make a call to London.

'Check a woman called Alix Johnston on Flight 477 from Heathrow yesterday,' he said when he finally got through. 'About five feet seven inches, fair, pretty, and seems about twenty-three. I'm changing my address. You can contact me at Sabri's from tomorrow.'

## CHAPTER SEVEN

It was, anyway, a friendly hotel for Sabri worked hard to see that his guests enjoyed themselves, but the communal balcony upstairs ensured extra close proximity. Alix, carefully tucking the passport Cary had given her into the bottom of her bag, glanced up and saw Jane through her open glass door. She was talking to the French couple who had moved into number seven. The couple walked back into their room and Alix said: 'Hi! Are you ready to go?'

Jane came over and as she did so her husband called: 'I'm locking the door, now.'

'Come through this way,' suggested Alix,

72

stuffing her travellers' cheques into the bag and adding a silk scarf to camouflage Cary's passport. Jane came in, locking the doors after her, and the two girls joined Brian in the corridor behind.

The car had been delivered earlier. It was a Fiat, not old in years but a victim of bad surfaces and changing drivers. 'I think she saw a lot of service before this road was sealed,' Brian remarked as she raged up the steep hill, coughing asthmatically, the bodywork rattling.

'When was the road sealed?' Jane asked flicking her head round.

'I haven't a clue.' Why ask me, Alix nearly said, but suddenly the Langleys were looking rigidly ahead in a silence that was electric as when one waits for a reply to a question that should not have been asked. Then Brian said: 'I must ask Sabri. I don't think it was too long ago,' and the queer, strained moment passed so that Alix thought she had imagined it.

They circled the town, skimming along the coast for a view of Mouse Island and the Monastery of Vlakhernes, both slumbering peacefully in the glass-smooth waters of the bay, then round by the twin Venetian forts, along the waterfront and into the mellow old town. 'Where shall we park?' Brian asked and Alix had again that queer, muddled feeling that his question was loaded.

Jane said: 'We have to go to the post office for mail, so let's leave the car somewhere near it.'

'I have to go to the post office, too,' Alix remarked without thinking.

'Got your passport?' Langley asked.

'Yes.'

Jane half-turned, resting an elbow on the back of her seat. 'You haven't brought your passport, Alix.'

'What! But I have. I put it in very carefully.' She patted her string shoulder bag reassuringly.

'No, dear. You left it on the dressing-table. I saw it when I came through your room.' Jane was looking gravely into Alix's startled face. 'I was going to suggest you either brought it or put it away, and somehow the moment passed.'

'Damn!' Of course it was Cary's false passport in her bag. She had been so concerned with its placing, concealing it carefully with the silk scarf, that she had completely forgotten her own.

'But is it important?' Jane asked. 'Surely you don't expect mail so soon? I mean you only came yesterday.'

The car swung up through a narrow lane of gaunt Renaissance houses. A quick decision to ignore the question about the mail, then: 'I need my passport for changing money,' Alix said. She would have to get

74

away from the Langleys to collect Cary's mail now, and that was going to be a complication.

The doctor manoeuvred the car into a space in the square, turned off the engine and said: 'I can give you a loan.'

Alix had enough for the swimming gear, but not enough for Benjamin's food. 'That's terribly kind of you. I really would be grateful.'

He opened his wallet and handed her some notes. 'Seven hundred drachmas. That's in the region of ten pounds.'

'Thanks awfully. I hope Sabri can change travellers' cheques.'

'If he can't, one of the big hotels will.' They locked the car and went into the post office together.

'Do you want stamps?' Langley asked.

'I'll get them at the kiosk when I get the cards—if I get cards,' Alix replied, keeping all channels open, and looking round, mentally noting the position of the *Poste Restante* grille. They walked off together and found a shop where Alix bought flippers and mask. There was a bookshop, and foodstores.

She had no idea anyway, at the moment, how she was going to hide a chicken. Certainly it would not go into her string bag, but she might be able to conceal it beneath the swimming gear. What she had taken on had seemed simple enough yesterday with Benjamin's need feathering her mind, but she realized now she should have turned down the Langleys' kind offer of a ride and hired one of those funny little motor scooters she had seen a man offering outside the Scheria. They wandered through to the old town, looking at the little jewellery shops and souvenir kiosks and boutiques. She bought a crocheted shawl for Lucilla and the Langleys bought gifts for their children. Towards mid-day they went through the arches to the town square.

'Ginger beer,' said Alix hopefully. 'I believe you can still get it here, ice-cold in stone bottles.' She leaned back in her chair looking across a promenade at tall green trees, a grass sward, a row of parked cars. 'This must be where they play cricket. That is if we're sitting in the Liston and I think we must be because it was modelled on the Rue de Rivoli, and see these wonderful old colonnades! Isn't this the Rue de Rivoli incarnate!' she exclaimed delightedly.

Brian gave her a quizzical look and Jane said a little crossly, brushing back the hair that had fallen damply round her face: 'Isn't it hot! I've never seen the Rue de Rivoli. I wish that waiter would hurry up. *Aloli! Mañana!* Mention of ice-cold ginger beer has made my mouth feel like the Sahara.' It had also taken away her tolerant holiday mood.

She flopped back in her chair, wiping her face. Brian looked round good-humouredly for a waiter. Jane's looks did not stand up well against neat and elegant women like Alix, but for him her faintly untidy air, her rounded bigness, gave her extra femininity.

Alix, sitting tautly upright, trying not to appear to be on edge, felt rebuked, but Jane's irritability gave her an opening of sorts. She said: 'You seem to be settled here for a while. I am sure you'd like to chat on your own. I'll have another quick glance at the shops.'

'Okay. We'll wait for you here.' Alix picked up the plastic bag containing the swimming gear.

'Don't cart that. We'll look after it,' Langley said.

Alix hesitated, flushed, then put it down again. Where was she going to hide the food, if not under this bulky stuff?

'What's the matter?'

'I thought—if I buy something—'

'Good lord, they'll give you another bag.'

She was not going to get away with this, she thought nervously as she went back through the archway into the town. They were bound to ask her what she had bought and in such a friendly, holiday atmosphere she was bound to tell them. On a package tour, with her meals paid for, they would think her crazy to be buying food. And as to

children's books and/or comics, they were
certainly not holiday souvenirs. But she had
to do it. She could not let Benjamin down.
She would buy the stuff, then work out how
to camouflage it.

She hurried back the way they had come,
then turned down a narrow street that
probably led towards the port. There were
no provision shops here. And she had not
passed a book shop. A narrow alley on her
right gave off delicious smells. Dear life!
How could she hide the scent of a newly
roasted bird? She hurried down the alley,
and paused outside a shop where chickens
were turning slowly on a spit. Behind, there
was a grocery store. She went up to the
counter. 'Do you speak English?' The Greek
nodded. 'I want a cold, cooked chicken.'

'Okay.' He picked up a bird from a tray
below the spit.

'That's not cold.' Unintentionally, her
voice was sharp, a protest.

'Is cold,' he retorted indignantly. 'If very
cold is not fresh. Cook today.' He wrapped it
swiftly in a very inadequate square of paper
and dropped it into a large plastic bag. Alix
touched the sides. 'Is cold,' said the man
firmly. It was very warm indeed for the heat
came through the plastic and it smelled as a
newly cooked chicken ought to smell,
delicious and with a fragrance that was not
going to be contained within this open-

topped bag.

Alix paid and the man gave her change then watched her with puzzled, faintly hostile eyes as she went round the shelves in search of the sort of food Benjamin might like. Biscuits and tinned rice pudding. Some jelly, and in the cool-box a plethora of fruit yoghurts and crème caramel. She bought recklessly.

Out on the pavement again Alix looked down with a grim sort of despair at the two big plastic bags she was now carrying. And there were still books and toys to add to this load! Next door was a dry cleaners, then an exotic little sweet shop with the air outside full of the scent of roasting almonds: a perfumery. This old part of the town was not going to supply her needs. And how long would it take her to run to the new part?

Back in the square Jane was saying to her husband: 'I think you may be right. I think she has been here before.'

He was pensive a moment. 'Yes, she obviously knows a lot about the island. But it's none of our business.'

'What? If she's Dora Johnston? No, I suppose not. But it crossed my mind that *he* might be here.'

Langley looked startled. 'Good Lord, whatever gave you that idea?'

'She's sort of, I don't know, jumpy sometimes. And for such an obviously very intelligent girl, she muddles things. Gives odd answers, and stops to think when there's no apparent reason why she should. Haven't you noticed?'

'Mmm. I'm not sure.'

'What I was going to say—I wish I had looked at that passport.' Jane caught her lip between her teeth and glanced up at her husband uncertainly. 'Would it become our business if we discovered she was hiding him here?'

Brian took a cigarette and lit it. 'You won't find that out from the passport. Let's wait and see what turns up, shall we?' Cary Johnston, according to the Press, had absconded with a lot of money that did not belong to him, but there was no reason to assume his wife had had anything to do with his crimes.

Down in the new town Alix raced across the square, the plastic bags bumping and lurching in her hands. The box containing the toy train speared her knee with the thrust of the weighty books behind it. 'Ouch!' She lost her balance, then fortunately regained it as she was about to fall. There was only one way out of this dilemma. If St. Spiridon of Corfu was on her side, the car boot would be unlocked. If not ... She grasped the catch and miraculously, it opened. She squeezed the air from the bag round the chicken and twisted it tightly, then scrabbled hopelessly in her string bag for a rubber band. The silk scarf! She tied it carefully round the neck of the bag. Ignominious treatment for an expensive Christmas present, she thought grimly as she jerked the scarf into a knot. She tucked the parcels carefully into a corner, superstitiously crossed her fingers, then closed the boot and dashed to the post office, taking Cary's passport out of her bag as she ran. Up the steps and across the floor to the grille marked *Poste Restante.* She presented the little black folder. The man behind the grille looked at the name, swung round to the pigeon-holes, swung back and slid the passport across.

'No. Nothing.' Alix picked up the passport and stuffed it guiltily into her bag. She was too concerned about getting back to the square to consider the implications of Cary having received no message from Dora. She ran across the big room and the squeak and shush of her sandals on the marble, together with the hum of talk from people in the room, was enough to drown the clerk's call: 'Fuller! Mrs Fuller!' She ran down the steps and sped back across the square, along the busy streets, across intersections and in and out of the alleys until eventually she was through the old town and heading for the main square.

'I hope she hasn't got lost,' Brian was saying concernedly, looking at his watch.

'It's after half past twelve now!'

Suddenly Alix appeared under the archway, panting and holding a hand to her side. Her face was scarlet, her hair clinging in damp tendrils to her forehead. She smiled apologetically as she came up to them. The arcade was alive with people now, tourists and locals alike, and the air was full of their chatter.

'Terribly sorry,' she apologized when she could get her breath. She collapsed into her chair. 'I got lost.'

'Where on earth did you go?'

'Heaven alone knows. Old town, new town. I'm an idiot about directions. Anyway, I found my way back at last.'

'And didn't you buy anything, after all that?'

There was a nerve-racking silence. 'No, er, no, I didn't.' After the rushing and the worry, she could not gather her wits. Guilty and vulnerable, she sat for a timeless moment while they stared at her. Then:

'We've got your drink but it's not very cold now,' Jane remarked reprovingly.

'D'you mind if I gulp? I'm dehydrated. I've been running for ever and heavens, it's hot!'

'You shouldn't have run,' said Jane, looking at her thoughtfully. 'We would have waited. But we were worried about you.'

Alix delved in her bag for a tissue and

wiped her face. She looked round for a waiter. 'That drink scarcely touched bottom. I shall have to have another. And by the way, these are on me.' She smiled across the table at Langley. 'On your money, of course. Your loan.'

They allowed her to pay. Walking back to the car, crossing by the steps of the post office, Brian remarked: 'You got your stamps all right with your postcards?'

'I didn't get any cards, as a matter of fact.'

She was thinking wryly how fate can sometimes hand one a useless miracle, and wondering if it would have occurred if she had really needed an excuse to go in alone for Cary's mail. Two young men were running down the steps in the bright sunlight. One of them caught her eye, stopped, turned back, staring at her. 'Mrs Fuller?' Her heart nearly stopped beating. She stared back at him, stricken. He must have taken her silence for assent. He said: 'I was at the *Poste Restante* grille when you came in. I am sorry, but there was some mail. I called out as you left but you did not hear.' The man hurried away.

'He called you Mrs Fuller,' said Jane in a strange voice. They were both looking at her as though she had materialized out of the air.

Alix gave a nervous little laugh. 'Someone looks like me,' she said. 'After all, I think I will dash in quickly and get some stamps

83

before they close. There are postcards at Sabri's.' She left them and hurried up the steps, glad to turn from their suspicious eyes. She had changed her mind too suddenly and too opportunely. The Langleys were not stupid. Her nerves were tight as violin strings as she handed the passport over the counter, not daring to look behind in case, out of sheer curiosity, the Langleys had followed her in. She took the letter handed to her and stowed it carefully in her bag, then walked slowly back to the door. She had only just made it. A man was waiting to lock up the building for the afternoon.

Back at the car she said lightly: 'Got my stamps.'

They were both staring at her, not believing her, waiting for her to unleash the mystery.

'Why didn't you ask for mail when we were here before? When you came in with us?'

'Because of having no passport. But I came across this square when I was lost and I decided, after all, I would nip in and ask, thinking I might talk them into bending the rules.' Alix said it with total calm, a sort of resignation to exposure.

They looked at her queerly and she knew they wanted to say again: 'But who is writing to you? You only arrived yesterday. The letter would be written before you left.' She turned away from their curious eyes, not wanting to lie and saying to herself. 'It's none of their business. Absolutely none of their business, and anyway, why should they care?' Then she remembered Cary and her commitment to the child. She must not leave ends open. She must not give anyone an opportunity to interfere. 'Actually,' she said, the colour coming up in her cheeks like fire, 'I was expecting a letter. But not from home. There was someone coming to meet me, from Athens. He said he would send a message to me here.'

They turned away. Langley unlocked the car. He was thinking the arrival of another man would put her friend Paul's nose out of joint. Then he caught his wife's eye. He slid in behind the wheel. He had never thought people were dumped on earth to enjoy themselves. But he sometimes thought they were here to help one another. The hurdles for some were considerably higher than for others. It was how one jumped that mattered, in the final evaluation. He and Jane weren't God. He had better have a talk with her.

# CHAPTER EIGHT

There was little conversation on the way back to Paleocastritsa. Brian made an effort as they ran down into the bay. 'What does Paul Crispin do?' Now that there was talk of another man, true or false, and the very real possibility that they were involved with the notorious financier's wife, Crispin seemed less of a delicate subject.

'I've no idea. I didn't talk to him much on the plane. He seems busy. Why?'

'I don't know. Just curiosity. I'm always interested in what people do and most people are quite happy to tell you, but he seemed very unforthcoming.'

'Did you ask him? I thought perhaps—property.'

'No. I didn't actually ask him. Not outright. He changed the subject before I got there, if you know what I mean.'

Alix did. Paul had done the same with her. But she was not particularly interested. She liked his company and she hoped he would come back. Spiro was there in front of the hotel, tempting passers-by with his bucket of lobsters. The waiters, black clad and bow-tied, moved between the restaurant and the road.

'Why don't you park back there,' Alix

suggested, pointing, suddenly realizing that if the car was uphill from the hotel she would have a better chance of removing her parcels undetected. 'It's a pity to spoil the view from the dining-room with cars,' she added swiftly as the doctor reached out to turn the engine off.

'You're right. Would you girls like to get out while I back?'

They climbed out. 'Thank you so much, Jane. It was awfully kind of you to take me, and I do appreciate it.'

'Delighted to have you.' The warmth that had been there before was replaced by an automatic politeness.

Alix paused at the top of the steps, looking back with apprehension as Langley locked the car and put the key in his pocket. Of course there was no reason why he should look in the boot, or even think to lock it, since he had not done so in the town. And then, inexplicably, he went to the boot and tried the catch. He took the key out of his pocket and locked it. Alix went along to her room, feeling shaken. Had they known, all the time? Or had the locking of the boot been a mere automatic action that had not been triggered off in the town? She threw her swimming gear down on the floor and opened the glass doors, wondering what on earth she was going to do. She had to get the keys quickly because the food had already been over long under the sun-hot metal shield of the car body.

'Hallo,' said a friendly, familiar voice and she looked up to see Paul standing on the balcony, a glass in his hand.

'How did you get there?'

'I couldn't resist it, after last night. I've moved in.'

It was what she had wanted, more than anything else, and yet his presence was going to make her contacts with Cary more of a complication than they had been before.

'Come over to my room and I'll pour you a drink of my duty-free.'

She stepped on to the balcony and followed him. He was wearing blue linen trousers and a very well tailored shirt with unusual stitching. His room was four doors along. 'There's a French couple next door,' he said, 'and a Dutch couple next to the Langleys. Sabri's is filling up. What do you want? Vodka?'

'You've a good memory. Yes, please.' He put his own glass down beside an empty one on the table. 'Heavens! Cut glass!'

'I gave up drinking spirits out of tooth glasses a long time ago,' Paul replied with a lively grin. 'Someone gave me this splendid little leather case and I take it everywhere.'

'What do you do if you have more than one guest?'

'They get the tooth glasses. They're used

88

to them.'

They laughed together, softly, almost conspiratorially, as though it was the middle of the night instead of the middle of the day. They wandered out on to the balcony just as Langley opened his double doors.

'Hi there! Back again!'

'It's the food,' said Paul. 'After last night's dinner I decided I couldn't tolerate my five star hotel in Corfu.'

'You mean you've moved in?'

'Two doors along.'

'Oh, great.' He gave Alix a whimsical look that said he did not really think Paul's arrival had anything to do with the food. Through the open doors Alix could see the car keys on the dressing-table. 'We're off to lunch,' Langley said.

Alix held her breath, waiting to see if he would shut the doors. He did not, and the breath eased out of her in a long, silent sigh. Still, there was a chance he might put the keys in his pocket. If he did, she would have to ask for them quite straightforwardly at lunch. It would be easy enough to say she had left something, though he had probably checked the interior of the car and knew well enough that she had not.

The Langleys looked up as they descended the steps. 'Aren't you eating?'

'Indeed. I'll be down when I've tidied up.'

'Keep us a seat,' said Paul.

She had to get him into his room so that he would not see her enter the Langleys' door. She emptied her glass fairly quickly and walked inside, putting it down on the dressing-table. He came in behind her and slid his arms round her waist, turning her to face him.

'Paul!'

'Never take chances with red-blooded men,' he said lightly, but his eyes were watchful. The business side of him was summing up her reaction. 'A girl with her wits about her would have handed me the glass outside.' She looked beautiful like this with her cheeks flushed. Not from embarrassment. She was too sophisticated for that. Yet she was nervous.

'Thanks for the tip.' She manoeuvred herself free. Certainly she knew all the tricks, but when one's mind was overfull with a plan to steal keys and remove a couple of large parcels, undetected, from someone else's car, there was scarcely a chance to remember to keep out of a man's room when his hands were empty. If, indeed, one wanted to.

'I'll see you downstairs. I have to change.' She shot through the door, checked outside the Langleys' room that it was still empty, ducked in, grasped the keys tightly in one damp hand and ran to her own room. Out the door and down the passage. So long as the Langleys were on the dining terrace it did not matter who saw her now. She sped down the steps and along the road. The key turned. She grasped the two big plastic bags, slammed the boot shut and, without bothering to lock it, sped back into the hotel. Paul met her on the steps.

'I see you've been spending money.'

'Just some underwater gear.' She brushed past him, taking the steps two at a time, dashed breathlessly along the passage, dropped the booty on her bed, shot out of the door and without thinking to look round, went straight to the Langleys' room. She dropped the keys on the dressing-table, spun about and as she emerged, pulled up involuntarily in shock. From the balcony rail the French couple were eyeing her suspiciously. She gave them something akin to a frightened grimace that was meant to be a smile, and entered her own room again.

Damn Cary! she said to herself angrily. She was not a natural for this sort of thing. And how she was going to get to him this afternoon with Paul's sharp eyes on her, she could not imagine.

She went into the bathroom and splashed her face with water, ran a comb through her hair and slipped out of the shirt and trousers she had worn in the town. It was cooler in the little slip of a dress she had worn yesterday and she felt calmer now. She went down to lunch, hurrying. At the bottom of the steps she checked, and assuming an air of dignity and comparative idleness, wandered across the dining terrace. I have to get used to acting, she thought. People stared at her as she came in alone, recognizing her for the girl Sabri had danced with last night.

The hot pink flowers of the bougainvillaea that ran up the cane sticks to form a summer wall for the terrace made a dramatic back-cloth for the brightly dressed diners. They framed a pretty face and made it beautiful. They loaned glamour to the swarthy Greek boys who waited on the tables.

Paul was saying: 'You're a different girl from the one on the plane. The air and the sun have got at you.'

Jane said to Brian: 'She obviously did get the letter from Athens. She's been different since that odd business outside the post office. Sort of relieved and excited. I wonder why she was so funny about it?'

'Embarrassment. Dead husband. New boyfriend. And the old one turning up.'

Jane smiled. 'I suppose this sort of thing happens all the time to pretty girls with a figure like hers.'

Alix was indeed functioning in top gear. Half of her was dealing hungrily with the lobster, the other half was dealing with the problem of how to get away tactfully after lunch, and through it she was vibrantly aware that she was being watched. That French couple who had seen her exiting from the Langleys' room. The woman looked hostile. She had to be ready with an excuse, and heaven knew where she would find one. The Langleys were far too interested in her now for comfort. And Paul. She had known almost immediately when they met that she could fall in love with him. She had, even in the plane, felt inexplicably drawn to him and each parting was harsh, like the jerking of a subliminal umbilical cord. Lucilla would say we had met before—help! Wasn't that what Paul had said? And she had thought him stylish and slick in his approach!

Paul broke into the pattern of her thoughts. 'You've a very expressive face and it's not saying: "What a terrific lobster!" What suddenly came out of your mind to astonish you?'

Quite truthfully, she replied: 'I am astonished at the way the holiday has turned out.'

'What did you expect?'

'A rather lonely lie in the sun.'

'Do you live with your parents?' he asked unexpectedly.

'They died when I was quite young. I have a guardian aunt. Or had. I'm a bit past guardians, now.'

93

'Is that why you married the boss's son? I'd guess there was a father figure there somewhere. And your building up the business after. Devotion to the interests of the father figure?'

'Guilt,' she replied. She put her knife and fork down and looked up at Paul, astonished at herself, yet not ashamed or even embarrassed.

He grinned. 'What did you do? Empty the petty cash box?'

She laughed. There was suddenly a queer, happy feeling of total release, as though Paul had unlocked a door on the past. 'I married the man who let the business run downhill.'

'Why didn't you stop him?'

'I was young, then. And he didn't want me in the office. In the two years I was married to Tim I grew up a lot and at the same time a good deal of the management talk was seeping in. I learned the business in a broad sense because I was no longer involved with petty detail. I found myself with a background of knowledge that even surprised me. And also, it was a hole in the ground for hiding my head. Tim died in England when we should have been here in Corfu. And it was my decision not to come here.'

'Ah!' If what she said was true it might be an explanation of the highs and lows in her as though some inner pendulum swung

94

between tension and release. Between a desire for solitude and a bursting balloon of self-expression. What he was seeing was a lively extrovert making tentative little forays through the shadows of the past. And then his clinical, cynical brain took over. He had met many expert liars in his field of business. Until he heard from London or managed somehow to get hold of her passport, he could not discount the possibility that she was Dora Johnston. Her behaviour could add up to that, too. And he had better control this feeling that was creeping over him in her presence. Something unfamiliar and disturbingly whole.

'What are you going to do this afternoon? I am considering a swim. And you've missed yours so far today, foraying into town.'

'Don't tell me you're not working,' she hedged.

'Not.'

'Oh.' She picked up a lobster claw in her fingers, broke it with a sharp crack. 'I was thinking seriously of a siesta.'

'You're joking!'

'No. It's the norm here.' She looked up at him innocently, sucking the sliver of white flesh out of its scarlet tube. 'And then perhaps a swim and a walk.'

'I was proposing to sunbathe for the first hour.'

'Oh, it's far too hot for me now.'

'I'll tell you what, then. I'll read on the balcony while you have the siesta, then we'll go to the beach together.'

'No, please. You got to the beach.'

'Don't look so horrified. It's great on the balcony. Such a magnificent view!'

He had warned her she had an expressive face. She would have to learn not to react to shocks. But how was she going to get down the steps and away from the hotel with Paul on the balcony?

The plan, when it came to her, was brash and there was no cover-up. She hated it because, more than anything else, she wanted his company. If she did it this way, he was going to assume she was avoiding him. He might even take the hint and leave the hotel. She looked up at him, at that curiously cheeky-boy smile in his rather tough face, and she felt suddenly desolate at the thought that he might go. As though he sensed a problem, he put a hand over hers, not caring that the tables were close together and anyone might see. Damn Cary, she thought fiercely, emotionally, seeing Benjamin's pale, lost face within its frame of unwashed hair. I'll do it this way, but it's only going to work if Paul sits with his back to the steps. And not so near that he hears my footfalls. And if he doesn't?

Dear God! I must organize it. I'll find a way.

# CHAPTER NINE

Alix reached the balcony first and moved the deck chair to the centre of the terrace, a few yards from her door. When Paul came out with a book in his hand she said: 'It's going to be very hot. Would you rather have it over by the rail? You might get a bit of a breeze there.' She edged the chair forward, its back to the steps.

Paul looked surprised. 'What service!'

He was now safely away from the end where the steps lay. It would have been so easy for him to drop into the chair wherever it happened to be. Now she had made him aware of position, there was a good chance he would stay anchored. 'You don't mind if I close my doors? It keeps the heat out.'

'Sure. What time shall I call you?'

'Say an hour?' That would give her plenty of time.

'Okay.' He sat down and opened the book.

It was going to be a long, hard climb up through the steeply terraced olive grove and Alix doubted if she could manage the almost vertical bit at the top with the impediment of a large plastic bag in each hand, but as she left the foot of the steps she saw a bus sitting at the end of the road by the beach. Even if it was destined for Lakones, to get aboard she would have to walk in front of the hotel. She sighed and set off up the hill, then turned left where the road forked. She had not gone more than a few yards when the bus came grinding after her. She stood on the edge of the road with the parcels at her feet, waving and smiling hopefully. Miraculously, the bus slowed to a halt and she climbed aboard.

★     ★     ★

Benjamin was sitting on a dry tussock at the side of the road making desultory marks in the dust with a stick. He had been there since early morning. Jani had brought the hard bread and goat's milk at breakfast time and Benjamin had gone back to the house with him, but Jani had not been able to stay because he had to go to school. Benjamin had tried once more to persuade his father to let him go to school with the other children, but he said: 'We'll be gone in a few days, son. It's not worth it. Anyway, Alix will be up today with something for you to play with.'

'Will she bring Mommy wif her?'

'Mommy can't come. I wish you wouldn't go on about her. Go and play quietly. I've got a headache. And remember what I said. Don't go into the village.'

So Benjamin had gone back to making lines in the dust by the big myrtle where the

98

white butterflies came. 'Don't go past the myrtle,' Daddy had said. He would have gone, though, if it had not been for Alix bringing the toys. He would have gone down to the forbidden bay to paddle and look at those funny little hermit crabs that Jani and Photini had taught him to catch. It was horrible at the little house with nothing to do and Daddy always cross. He wished Mommy would hurry up and come. She would take him to the beach and what's more, she would buy him a bucket and shovel at the shops.

There was a hole in the bracken directly behind. Benjamin crawled in and rolled around on the dry juniper needles and broken stalks. In the end there was a little bed. He lay on his back staring at the molten sky. Perhaps, if he found some sticks, he could make a proper house. He busied himself breaking off bramble stalks and laying them flat on top of the living fronds.

It was nice sitting in the fern house but that became boring too in the end so he went over to some stones covered in dry moss and pretended he was a king sitting on a throne. He wished he had some friends. Later, he wandered back to the house and crept quietly inside, but Daddy was asleep again. He climbed up on a box in the kitchen and got himself a drink of water. Then he wandered back down the road, threshing aimlessly at the bushes with a stick. Where was Alix? He kicked a cloud of dust all over himself, and at that moment Madame Dolli came with the tray on her head and scolded him for making a mess of himself.

'Come back, Spiro. Is lunch.'

'Alix is bringing me lunch.'

'Who is this Alix, heh?'

'She's my auntie.'

'Auntie, heh? You come.'

'No, I am waiting for Alix.' He sat down stubbornly at the side of the road again. If only Alix would come! If only Mommy would come.

It was hours later when he saw Alix coming round the corner with her big plastic bags and her happy, friendly smile. Benjamin leaped off the tussock, caught his feet in the dropped stick and sprawled headlong. She ran to him, abandoned her parcels and picked him up. 'Oh Benjamin! Are you hurt?'

He was too excited to cry. He lifted his grubby face, buttoned tightly against a wail, the eyes brimming. 'No, I'm all right. Did you—did you bring the toys?'

'Yes, I did. But oh dear! Do let me dust you down. What a mess! And your hair! I'll tell you what. In exchange for the presents, will you let me wash your hair?'

'There's no bafroom.' He edged towards the parcels as Alix beat the dust gently out of his clothes.

'I can do it without a bathroom. Shall we go to the house before we open the parcels? Everything in this packet is for you. Books, toys, comics.'

'Can I carry it?' His small hands, ingrained with dirt, were already closing on the handle.

'Sure, and everything in this packet is for you, too. A chicken.' She gave him a conspiratorial look and he hunched his shoulders and gave her back a shy little grimacy smile.

'I frowed it away like you told me.'

'That's a good boy. It was nice of you to come and meet me.'

He did not answer. He was hurrying as fast as his short legs and the weight of the booty would allow down the track that led to the house, with the plastic bag bumping against his knees and feet. The door was open and they went straight in. 'Cary,' she called. There was no reply.

'Can I open it now?'

'Yes, of course.'

The bedroom door was open. Cary was spread-eagled on the bed. The mean little room smelled hot and airless.

'Cary! What's the matter? Are you ill?'

He raised himself on one elbow. 'Ah! There you are! Did you get any mail?'

'Yes, I did. A letter with a London postmark but I'm sure it's not from Dora,

101

it's addressed in a very masculine hand. But what is the matter, Cary?' His dark hair was damp and his face flushed. The perspiration had come through his shirt and his eyes were hazy.

'I'm perfectly all right,' he said, putting his feet to the floor. She noticed apprehensively that he paused a moment before standing up.

'But you're not all right. You're ill!'

'I've had a bit of a temperature, that's all. I'll be all right.' He raised the lid of his suitcase and pulled out an expensive looking sweater. A passport that had been wrapped inside fell among the jumble in the case. He pushed it out of sight. So he carried his own papers as well as those of the fictional Mr Fuller! She went on out to the living-room and he followed. 'Where's the letter?'

Benjamin was seated on the floor, watching ecstatically while a tiny engine romped across the tiles.

'Where's the letter?' repeated Cary.

She delved into the carry-all and handed it to him. 'That's Dora,' he said, scarcely glancing at the address. He slit the envelope and sat down to read. She settled on the floor beside Benjamin while Cary read. The child leaned his head against her.

'Will you read me a story?'

She reached for a book. 'One story, then the hair wash. Okay?'

Benjamin nodded. He put both hands round her arm and rested his head on them. 'Will you stay with us?'

'For a little while.'

'Tonight. Stay tonight. Daddy will let you.'

'I'd like to, really I would, darling, but there's nowhere to sleep.'

'You can sleep with me. I don't mind.'

'You're very kind to ask me to stay, but I have to go back to my hotel.'

'Why?'

Alix put both arms round him. 'I'll come and see you every day,' she said.

He sighed deeply. 'Where's Mommy?'

'I expect she'll come soon.' Cary had gone back to the bedroom. 'You go on playing with your train for a moment,' she said, 'while I speak to your father.'

Cary was lying down again. She went swiftly to the bedside and looked down at him in deep concern. 'What had Dora to say?'

'Nothing useful,' he said. 'At least they haven't forgotten me.'

'Who? Who hasn't forgotten you?'

He made no reply. His eyes were closed. 'Look here,' she said, 'I can't leave you like this. You're ill.'

He did not even bother to open his eyes. 'No I'm not. Just a bit under the weather.'

'Cary, there's a doctor at the hotel—'

His eyes flew open and he sat up with a jolt. '*No!*'

'I could swear him to secrecy. Doctors don't tell tales.'

'No!' Cary replied violently. 'I will not have anyone come here.' She was thinking that she would bring Langley if she had to, and perhaps he saw it in her eyes for he jerked forward, grasping her by the hands. 'If you're going to meddle, then get out and stay out.'

The violence of his reaction had shaken her rigid. 'And what happens to Benjamin if you get really ill?'

'He's not your problem, Alix!'

But he was her problem and would go on being so until he was re-united with his mother. Cary saw through her distress to that fact and changed his tactics. He ran his hands up her bare arms and pulled her down on the bed beside him. 'You're all Benjy and I have here,' he said gruffly. 'Don't let us down.'

Sitting close, Alix was appalled by the heat of his body, his wet face, and the rank sweat that had already broken through the cashmere sweater.

She plucked up courage to say: 'That letter wasn't from Dora, Cary. Why won't you confide in me?'

He pulled her roughly, hedonistically, so that she lost her balance and fell into his

104

arms. The sweat from his face brushed a film of moisture across hers and because her arms were pinioned she was unable to resist when he kissed her, wetly, unpleasantly. She struggled uselessly, without prop or balance, her feet flailing the air. 'Cary, let me go!'

'No. You could love me if you let yourself. Love us both,' he added as a quick, sly afterthought.

'I could bite you,' she threatened angrily, 'and I shall.'

'Little devil. Daring little devil.' He pushed her back so that he could look into her eyes. 'You're right, that letter was not from Dora. Dora's a bitch,' he said. 'She doesn't care two hoots in hell for either of us.'

Through the open door came the tinkle and buzz of the toy train. Alix, her arms freed at last, broke away. She stood up, shaking her short dress to rights, smoothing her hair, wiping her hand across her mouth then holding it there as though to block out the obscenity of Cary's kiss, hating herself for being disturbed by his intolerable likeness to Tim. By his frightening masculinity.

She said, her voice shaking: 'If I am to help you, you will have to tell the truth, Cary.' She had never been able to cope with lying. Lies threw her, and they angered her, too. Emotionally disturbed by events, she remembered with an unpleasant shock how

105

she had lied to the Langleys in Corfu. At the time, it had seemed more of an embarrassment to be telling them she had a rendezvous with another man, than the fact that she lied. Well, people in trouble lied. She looked down at Cary with a return of compassion.

'Dora has thrown in the sponge. Of course I didn't want to tell you. I hadn't faced up to it myself.'

When she should have been sympathizing with him, she found herself wondering what he had done to Dora that she should let him down like this. 'When did you hear?' she asked.

'It's in this letter. And there are rumours that I am here. The airport may be watched. If I am to get away, it will have to be by boat.'

'Where would you go, if you could get a boat?'

'North Africa.'

'Have you committed an extraditable offence?'

He said: 'I haven't *committed* anything. You know that. I'm in a mess, that's all.'

'Cary, if you are truly innocent why not come back and face up to an enquiry? British justice—'

'British justice my foot!' he retorted harshly. 'My so-called creditors would be after me like a pack of wild dogs.'

# CHAPTER TEN

She was puzzled about his saying the airport was being watched. If he had not committed an extraditable offence, then there was no extradition order, and did it matter who was watching the airport?

'Cary, you have said the Greeks are helpful and friendly. Would you allow me to bring a local doctor to you? What about the woman who cooks for you?'

'Okay,' Cary agreed weakly. He seemed no longer to care.

'What is the woman's name?'

'Dolli Vassilakis. She's at this end of the village. When you turn the last corner, just before you come to the square where the look-out is, there is a narrow lane going up on the left. Hers is the third house. Benjamin can take you there.'

Alix went back into the living-room. Benjamin was down on his knees winding up his train. He looked up, saw Alix. 'Read me a story now?'

'Not just at the moment, darling. We have to go and see Madame Vassilakis.'

'Why?' he asked suspiciously. 'You brought the dinner.'

'It's nothing to do with food.'

He beamed up at her then. 'I looked in the

other bag. You brought me some custard. Yum-m.'

'Daddy is sick and Madame Vassilakis can get a doctor for him.' Benjamin scrambled to his feet. She took his hand and led him out of the front door. 'You can show me the way.' Benjamin skipped along the track beside her, raising dust with gleeful little kicks.

They came up towards the look-out. 'When you turn the last corner before the square...' Cary had said. Across the square, seated on the wayside bench where she had drunk her beer in the heat of the previous day, sat Paul Crispin! He had come looking for her! The awareness filled her with a tingling sensation of fright, and joy, and fear.

'We're not there,' said Benjamin, straining against her as she pulled him urgently into the bushes at the side of the road.

Trying hard to keep the anxiety out of her voice, Alix said: 'Let's have a game. Let's pretend there's an Indian in the square looking for us.'

'An Indian?' Benjamin sounded astonished.

'No, well, maybe not. A Dalek?'

'Oh, yes!' he exclaimed delightedly. 'Yes, a Dalek.'

'Now, there's a lane we want to get to over there in front and on the left.' She tried to smile but her face was tight as parchment.

'There's a Dalek in the square and he mustn't see us.'

'No, he mustn't see us,' agreed the child, entering enthusiastically into the spirit of the game.

'So ... if we dive through this scrub, maybe we'll find a way up the side of the hill. Hold my hand.' There was wild parsley and fennel here, a rose that tore at her dress; a dwarf juniper, a bed of the deep green scented maquis. The thorny rose had missed Benjamin by a hair's breadth. He said plaintively: 'I fink perhaps the Dalek has gone home now. Let's go back to the road.'

She picked him up in her arms. 'No, this is fun. Hold on to me tightly, darling, because there are some brambles here and I need one hand to push them off.' The way was harder going than she had expected. She caught her feet on stones, invisible beneath the low brush, stumbled forward, regained her balance and forged on. A great bramble sucker broke free and dealt her a stinging slap. Benjamin gave a shriek and tightened his arms round her neck. Alix soothed him gently. 'We're nearly through. I can see a clearing in front.'

They came to a stone wall. Alix lifted the child over. Ahead now were the backs of the houses in the lane where Madame Vassilakis lived. The third house up, Cary had said. Painted dark green with a red door and

109

window. She could see it from here, but there was no gate in the stone wall that ran across the back. They would have to climb over the top. They crossed a wild piece of ground where mallow, vetch and thistle grew. Benjamin had recovered his good spirits.

'Now, this looks like Madame's little house.' She lifted Benjamin on to the wall, then clambered over herself and helped him down. They were in a wild garden where white anemones with black centres grew, and the scent of honeysuckle lay thickly on the air. There was a patch of vegetables—big cabbages, tight as footballs, and melons in flower; potatoes, and the blue-green of onion stalks. They walked up the narrow path and Benjamin knocked timidly on a wooden door that stood ajar.

The door was opened immediately by a surprised woman with a brown face and black hair. She spoke to Benjamin in Greek, and he mumbled something in return, looking back in pink embarrassment at the garden, and then up into Alix's face for help. 'I am sorry,' she said. 'Mr—' she stopped dead, staring with startled eyes and empty brain into the shrewd face of the Greek woman. What name did Cary use? Not, surely, his own? Fuller? 'The child's father is ill,' she said.

'Ill?'

'Yes. Could you find a doctor and bring him to the house?'

Madame Vassilakis nodded. 'I get docteur.' Briskly, she picked up a black head scarf that was hanging behind the door, then with a gesture indicated that Benjamin and Alix go through to the front of the house.

'Thank you. We will go back the way we came.'

'Is no gate. Here, in front is street,' the woman insisted, nodding her head forcefully. 'Come.'

Benjamin slipped into the kitchen and Alix leaped after him. 'Come, darling, we must go back the way we came. Thank you so much, Madame. We will wait for the doctor at the house.'

Madame Vassilakis watched from the doorway, eyes puzzled, while they made their exit. Paul was still there at the look-out. With the child's hand tightly held in hers, Alix picked her way over the dry juniper needles, through the maquis and scrub oak and emerged at last beyond the corner and well out of sight of the square.

'Race you!' Benjamin cried and zoomed off down the road in a scatter of dust.

★     ★     ★

The doctor, when he came, was brisk, critical and curious. He stood in the front doorway looking round the bare little room in evident surprise. Alix, who had not heard his approach, lifted Benjamin down from her knee and rose to greet him.

'Please come in. Mr Johnston—' (Cary had said 'What the devil do you think I'm called? The locals know me.')—'Mr Johnston has a fever.' She led him into the bedroom, leaving them together. Through the door she could hear the two men talking in Greek. When the doctor emerged he was smiling. 'He is all right, Madame. Your husband has had a virus infection. But the worst is over. I have given him some pills, but it is rest he needs.' The doctor looked interestedly, critically, round the room. 'There are better houses you could have hired in Corfu, Madame.'

'Yes.'

'Even for a man in trouble—your husband has told me there are political troubles— there are places where one might stay discreetly hidden. Perhaps I could help you. In the more remote areas—'

Benjamin broke in with confused and damning innocence: 'Alix is not Daddy's husband.'

'Hush dear,' murmured Alix, then gave the doctor a stiff, pink smile.

'Ah!' Eyes twinkling, he looked her over with warm and particular interest.

Alix led him to the door. 'Thank you very

112

much for coming,' she said stiffly. 'Have you a car?'

'I had to leave it where the road narrows. Well, little boy, no doubt you are enjoying your rugged holiday. Eh?' and with that the doctor went briskly out of the door.

Alix returned to the bedroom. 'That was totally unnecessary,' she told Cary angrily. 'If I come across him and he asks me how my husband is, in front of people from the hotel—'

'Highly unlikely.' Cary brushed her protest aside. 'He won't go down to the beach.'

'It is possible for him to come to Sabri's for a meal,' she retorted tartly. 'And I am not living like a hermit, you know. I have made friends.'

He asked critically: 'Isn't that rather tricky?'

'Yes, it is,' she replied, thinking of Paul waiting at the look-out and wishing she could join him. 'It is very tricky. But I did not come to Corfu to look after you. If it was not for Benjamin, I'd—'

'Leave me flat?' Cary looked at her through narrowed eyes.

She said drily. 'I am becoming quite practised at picking up the pieces after the Johnston family. I dare say I can go on doing it a bit longer.'

'That's my girl.' Cary sat up in bed and

113

shook some tablets out of a small phial. 'I didn't actually say you were my wife. He assumed it. Get me a glass of water, will you? Tomorrow,' he said as he took the glass from her hand, 'I will be better and we can go for a picnic.'

'If you're sure you are going to be well enough to amuse Benjamin, I would like to spend my day on the beach. That's what I came here for. I would be delighted to take Benjamin with me, if you'll agree.'

'We've already talked about that.'

'You won't change your mind? I would not have to take him to Paleocastritsa.'

'No!'

Without consciously giving her mind to it, a plan had begun to form. What could Cary do if she abducted Benjamin? Absolutely nothing, if he was afraid to appear in public. She would have to think around this, for how could she take him to Sabri's now? 'You're not so ill you can't look after him tomorrow,' she told Cary. 'The doctor said you need rest, and Benjamin will be content with the toys and books I brought if you read to him. I have put plenty of food in the kitchen. I have washed his hair. And I have washed some very dirty clothes. Goodness knows if they are very clean, but the water was cold. Benjamin's tea is all ready.'

'That's good of you.' Cary put his feet to the floor. 'Are you going now?'

'Yes.' She hesitated. 'Cary, I thought of telephoning Dora.' She had not thought of it, until this moment. Without thinking out the plan to take Benjamin to Sabri's, the idea was falling apart in her mind. If anyone was interested in locating Cary, a Mrs Johnston with a newly acquired nephew was a pretty obvious sign. Especially to the Langleys, and Paul, who knew she had come here alone.

'I've told you. Dora has dropped us.'

'Not her child. No, Cary, I don't believe she would abandon her child.'

He stared down at his hands. His face was cold now, and hard.

'Let me ring her. Give me her number. I'll be terribly careful what I say.'

'But why do you want to talk to her?'

She sighed sharply, with exasperation. 'Because it's wrong to have the child here. You know it is. We could fix something up between us. You have been ill. What happens if he gets ill?'

'Why should he?'

She glanced into the living-room, then seeing Benjamin was down on the floor absorbed in his train, said soberly: 'Children die more quickly than men, Cary. That's why. And you don't know a damn thing about children.'

'I don't know where you would get hold of Dora now,' Cary replied. 'I've told you she has chickened out.'

115

'Maybe she had gone home, then.'

Cary lay back on the bed. 'I can't be bothered arguing with you. I'll be out of here soon and you can get on with your damned holiday,' he said curtly, his eyes closed.

She watched him for a moment. 'There is something you're not telling me, isn't there?'

'There's a lot I'm not telling you. But when I go, I'll leave the boy with you. Okay?'

'When are you going? How?'

'There is something in train. I'll let you know. I am going—shortly.'

She could not decide if he was telling the truth or if, not wanting her to ring Dora, he was soothing her with false hope. 'Promise?'

'Yes, I promise. I'll be able to let you know soon.'

She went into the living-room, bent down and kissed Benjamin, then taking her shoulder bag went to the door. 'See you tomorrow,' she said.


# CHAPTER ELEVEN

Paul left the car in the village street. There was no reason why Alix should recognize it. One hired car was much like another. He supposed the bus driver was telling the truth when he said he dropped her at the look-out. Unlike that fierce liar Sabri, he had no reason to shield her. Sabri's total preoccupation was for the comfort of his guests, and females first. If he had been able to turn Paul away without loss to the hotel's economy, as he had so artlessly pointed out, he would have done so. He did not like his men guests to bother the ladies and Mrs Johnston was a particularly lovely lady. If she had slipped away it would be because she wanted privacy and to that she was entitled.

Well, Paul thought now, this was a comfortable enough place to wait—and wait he would, until she turned up as she had to if she was returning to the Scheria.

Of course, he could go searching through the village or up and down the various tracks, but that way she had an eighty per cent chance of seeing him before he saw her. As a vantage point this seat was first class. All he need to know was the direction she came from. Besides, it was a very pleasant spot and the beer was cold.

Three beers later, his watchful eyes saw a flash of blue beyond the ilex tree. He knew when not to start, or raise his head. Alix had to come back this way because, foolish in her fright at seeing him, she had scuttled off the wrong side of the approach road and short of losing herself in the tree-clad hills that led down to the cliffs, she had no alternative. He ordered another drink, lit a cigarette and prepared to sit it out.

'A landscape which precipitates the inward crisis of lives as yet not fully worked out.' Alix had quoted those words last night as they stood on the balcony after the dancing. He had wondered what she meant but he had not been able to get the words out of his mind since. He knew, and he felt she knew, that something was going to happen. There was, in their silences, a subtle tension, an inevitability of attraction. Whatever had made her leave him flat this afternoon, it was part of this strangeness, a manipulation of the Gods.

He wished Barrington would get in touch. If she was Dora Johnston then the sooner he knew the better. The business side of him said he would smartly get uninvolved. If Cary Johnston was holed-up somewhere outside this village, it was not going to be too difficult to run him to earth. Or was it? These damned Greeks with their heritage of political razzamataz and their long love-affair with the British, their hatred of officialdom, would give him no help. And Cary Johnston, knowing them, would be quick to convince them he was in grave political strife. It was the only sort of trouble these peasants understood.

It took Alix half an hour to discover there was no escape. She wandered up the path that ran between the cypresses, looking nonchalant, with a little bunch of wild flowers in one hand. Paul watched her steadily, knowing if he stared hard enough she would have to turn round.

'Good lord! Fancy finding you here!'

She was no mean actress, he thought, watching her face light up with what appeared to be genuine pleasure.

'I've been waiting for you.' Then, observing her closely, he added with cool deliberation: 'I saw you come up that road over there, and I was getting up to go and meet you when you disappeared.' That shook her. He saw the almost imperceptible narrowing of her eyes, the caught breath, the stillness that is a preparation for shock. 'Where have you been?' he asked.

'Down towards the cliffs. I thought I might find a track leading back to the Scheria.'

Of course. Avoidance tactics! 'I meant, where were you before I saw you? What is down that road you came up originally?' He had risen to his feet and was watching her, half smiling, but with eyes as sharp as blades.

'Down that road? Nothing, really. It ends just round the corner. I mean, it narrows down to a track.' She turned back to look at him, her eyes sparkling and her voice warm, enthusiastic, and sweetly phony. 'I've been looking at the flora and fauna. I found a crab spider on a wild pink rose. I transferred him to a white rose and he went white as a pearl.'

'Alix!'

'And I found a tortoise with a scaly head and the most beady black eyes. Like onyx.' She was chattering to cover up, and it worked. All the suspicion fell away, leaving only enchantment, and behind it an agony of mind. He took her hand and led her to the table he had just vacated.

'I really thought you had gone to sleep beneath the cypress trees. I was going out to search for you, soon.'

'Oh no. Never that. Did you not know that the cypress is a thief of intelligence? If you go to sleep under them the roots will crawl into your brains and steal them and you will wake as mad as a hatter?'

He laughed delightedly. 'Is that an old peasant tale?'

She nodded gravely. 'Frightening, isn't it?'

'It is indeed. And now, it's apéritif time,' he said. The disappointment of finding her room empty, the following anger at her trickery, the long drawn out, cold determination of the wait, were suddenly another world, and he did not want to know why she had evaded him lest it be something he could not face. A waiter appeared from the café opposite in that lightning way Greek waiters come, and Paul ordered two ouzos. The sun was going down, the air cooling. Not a ripple disturbed the surface of the bay. A brilliant gold was spreading across the sky.

Paul said: 'I've tentatively hired a caique for tomorrow. Would you come with me for a little jaunt?'

She wanted to go, but she quelled the delight rising up in her and said uneasily: 'Where to?' Cary and Benjamin were well catered for. Why should she not go with him? The invisible thread between them tightened.

'There's a little island up the coast a bit. A lovely beach. Do come, I want to know you better.' At that moment he did not give a hoot in hell about the Light & Heyward Insurance Company, who were paying him to track down one of the sharpest, most diabolical financial brains to tangle with British law for many a day. He had to have this lovely girl. He would worry about the pitfalls and the hurdles when they came.

\*     \*     \*

Word had gone round that tonight the band would be at the Circe, a beach-side restaurant tucked snugly against the rocks on the curve of the bay across the isthmus from Sabri's.

'It moves around,' said Paul, 'and the keen dancers follow it. As the queen of Greek dancing, you'll be expected to turn up.'

Alix made a face. 'I am only queen when I have Sabri for king.'

121

'Tonight you shall have me for king.' Paul was standing outside her door looking in while she dried her hair after their swim.

'Shall I bring the glasses over and pour you a drink in here?'

'No thanks. That French couple are at the railing behind you and they're watching me like hawks.'

'I think Sir fancies you.'

She laughed. 'That's nice. I like to be fancied. Let's have a drink outside, anyway. My hair is about dry.'

The Langleys came out and joined them. Over the moonbright tree tops the bay gleamed silver and the cicadas beat out a night song in the thicket beyond. In the shadow of a gnarled grape vine the jade-green light of a firefly gleamed.

'This is the most romantic place I have ever been in,' Alix said softly.

Brian elbowed his wife and they wandered silently away. 'I think we're a little *de trop*, darling.'

Paul was saying: 'You quoted something last night that has stuck in my mind all day. About the landscape precipitating the inward crisis—'

'—of lives as yet not fully worked out.'

'What did you mean? Where does it come from?'

'Cato and Cicero. Cato was on his way to Italy to throw himself on Caesar's mercy.'

'I am sorry to appear so ignorant, but who were they?'

She looked down at the golden liquor in her glass and said softly: 'It doesn't matter. It seemed apt. For me.'

'It is apt,' he said soberly. 'Do you know how apt it is?' He put a finger beneath her chin and looked into her eyes, searching. She thought, not of him, but of Cary and not only his sweat-filled ardour that had so filled her with disgust, but also Tim's blue eyes that lived still, in his cousin. Eyes that had looked into hers too searchingly, flinging the past up in a wave that engulfed her in guilt. Tim, looking at her in Corfu where she had not wanted him to come that week-end he was killed. Something in her flinched. A shadow flickered across Paul's face and was gone. Then his hand dropped to his side. 'Let's go and eat, shall we?' he said.

\*     \*     \*

The Circe was packed. Not only was the band there tonight, but it was the proprietor's Saint's day and free wine was spilling from a great keg garlanded in vines. Paul and Alix had walked across the isthmus arm-in-arm, down the moonsplashed passageways between the olive trees. She had been gay over dinner. Gay and lively and feminine and foolish, so that once he said:

'Did someone walk over your grave up there on the terrace before?'

'Yes. I think so.'

'Has the ghost gone, now?'

'Yes.'

'Okay. I'll try to be careful.'

In its way, the little exchange was a frail pact and a beginning. It was not going to be easy for Alix to start again. And Paul knew he was staring blindly into a wall because he was afraid to look over. He had not asked her why she ran away this afternoon. The truth was over that brick wall and he was tall enough to see, if he jumped. In a way, he had handed over to Barrington. When Barrington's advice came, he would move because he had to.

They found a table outside, on an open verandah that ran the full length of the Circe and hung over the rocks with a view of the moonlit bay. The waiters here were dressed in dark trousers with open-neck shirts and scarlet cummerbunds. They shouted to each other over the sound of the music and chatter. One of the young boys who was helping came up to them. 'My name Georgio. You want wine? Is free tonight.'

Three yachts lay silently at anchor, still as the villas on their rocky hill. A cruiser was gliding to a mooring. In the bright moonlight they could see men in shorts hurrying to the bow. 'Let's dance,' suggested Paul, and leaving Alix's bead bag on the table as a reservation ticket, they moved over to a small dance floor that lay beneath a thatch. The Langleys were standing against the wall, watching. When the music stopped they were still standing in the same place. Alix went over to them. 'You haven't got a table?'

'No. It's full up.'

'Come and join us.'

'No, really.' Jane looked embarrassed. 'We don't want to intrude.'

'But you must.' Paul took her by the arm and they came, protesting. 'Our friend Georgio will bring some chairs.'

He brought stools and some more wine. There was a dinghy being lowered from the cruiser that had just come in. They watched it as the little outboard motor sprang to life and sent it winging across the glass-smooth water, the wash fanning out behind, white and frothy as spun lace. They tied up below the Circe and climbed the steps, a big, fair man who could have been English, or German; a dark haired, pallid-faced man with heavy shoulders; and a small, chunky Greek. Below, and a little to the left, there was a rock terrace set in the cliff where fish snacks were served. The men paused there, considering. A waiter came out with a menu and they drew together, reading it.

'Dance?' said Paul. 'Listen, the band has been joined by a flute. And they've started the Greek dancing over there.'

Alix leaped to her feet, spilling some of the wine from her glass on to the table. Who was that man? She had seen him somewhere before. He had something to do with Cary. The music was lively, the accordian and violins leaping to join the twirls and flourishes of the flute. She took Paul's left hand and one of the young Germans from the scuba-diving school came forward to grasp hers. They moved into a swaying, kicking line. She looked up and saw the three men who had come off the cruiser standing at the entrance. She could see the fair-haired man quite clearly now. Yes, there was that very distinctive birthmark above his right eye, and the slight cast; the crooked, long nose. Alix felt the nerves in her shoulders tense. The man's gaze darted round the company. It rested on her, caught her look. The music stopped.

'And about time.' Paul took out a handkerchief and wiped his brow. 'Thank heavens we've a table on the verandah away from this crowd.'

'You go on,' Alix said, her voice high and queer. 'I'll just see if there's a Ladies'.' She went towards the entrance where the three men stood. Paul went back to the verandah.

'Phew!' he said to the Langleys as he dropped back into his chair. 'How sensible of you to sit that lot out! What must it be like in

126

August?'

Jane said: 'I see Alix has met a friend.'

Alix was nowhere in sight. 'She went to the powder room, or whatever they call it here,' he said.

'She went up to those men who came in off the cruiser. They have gone out the door together. I thought she was looking as though she knew them, when they came up the steps.'

Paul sat back in his chair, staring at the table where Alix's handbag lay. A girl usually took her bag with her when she went to the powder room. His fingers reached out and touched it, the two middle fingers drumming at the beading. He said, without looking at the Langleys: 'There a rumour afoot that Cary Johnston is on this island. That's why I'm here.'

'We wondered,' said Brian.

Paul's fingers went on drumming at the bag. They were all staring at it now. The music began again. Brian said stiffly: 'One accepts you have a job to do. Come and dance, Jane.' They went off together.

Shielded by their movements as they rose to their feet, Paul slid the bag to his knee, flicked the catch open and swiftly drew out a passport-sized package wrapped in a handkerchief. 'Fuller!' He said the name out loud, explosively. There was a piece of tape holding the book shut. He hesitated, tried to lift it then gave up. 'Christ!' he muttered under his breath. 'What does this mean?' With his eyes on the door, he tightened the handkerchief round the passport, and slid it back into the bag. It did not make sense. If she had come here calling herself Fuller when her name was Johnston, it would be understandable. The other way round made nonsense of his suspicions. A queer, nervous sort of nonsense that set his heart singing, but only for a moment. The sober, alert business side of him was telling him to think around this. There had to be an explanation.

The French couple from room number seven were seated three tables away. 'Look!' exclaimed Marcel. 'Did you see the man Crispin open her bag? Cool as you like! Had a good look inside and put it back on the table again.'

'It seems to me they're a very peculiar lot,' his wife replied, sniffing. 'I don't think I'll bother to tell Mrs Langley that Mrs Johnston was in her room. It seems to me they're as bad as each other.'

The Langleys came back to the table. They sat down opposite Paul and looked at him with an uncomfortable, furtive air. He said: 'The name is Fuller. What do you make of that?'

'She picked up some mail in Corfu today addressed to Fuller.'

And then it was suddenly clear. So, she

had been delivering mail when she ran away this afternoon! And Cary Johnston, husband, relative, or perhaps in spite of the name quixotically only a friend, could be holed up down that road beyond the village of Lakones! There could not be more than one or two houses there. He'd have proof by lunch time tomorrow. And proof of Alix's identity, too. A shattered dream? He had better play it cool tonight. Because, if she did turn out to be Dora Johnston, she was going to be hard to forget.

## CHAPTER TWELVE

Alix could not remember his name, only that they had met before. She gave him an opportunity to recognize her first, standing in front of him for the odd moment too long so that all three men looked at her. Then she said: 'I am Alix Johnston. Are you not business associates of—' she suddenly realized that her voice had risen and she dropped it to a whisper, '—my cousin Cary.' His eyes narrowed. 'I believe we met at a party at Richmond Hill.'

'Let's go outside,' the fair man said curtly. There was no light beyond the entrance to the taverna, only the flakes of moonlight that had scattered through the trees. He gave her a none-too-gentle push and she went forward, the other two following behind.

'Isn't this far enough? I only wanted to ask you if you have come for Cary.'

The man did not reply, except to give a sort of grunt and push her on. There was a clearing here with several dog kennels. The dogs came up to them sniffing suspiciously, but did not bark. 'There's no need to go any farther,' Alix protested in alarm. They were already nearly a hundred yards from the Circe. 'Just out of sight,' said the man, taking her arm in a hard grip. They were now in a tiny farmyard sandwiched between houses and the low cliff. Two goats lay on the ground, tethered to a pole, and beyond, a donkey.

'Now, what's this?' asked the man. 'What's this about meeting me before?'

She could no longer see his face in the tree shadow, and she was scared. 'I don't remember your name, but you're an associate of Cary's. I wanted to ask if you had come for him.'

The man's head came down, his chin jutted out. 'Let's have it straight.'

The dark-haired man and the Greek stood behind. Little hairs began to creep upright on Alix's neck. 'I know he is here,' she said. 'I have been looking after them.'

'Them!' The word came like a pistol crack. 'Cary and his little boy. Have you come to take them away? Cary was expecting someone.'

'And how do we know who you are?'

'I've told you.'

'So what are you doing here?'

His staccato questions, punctuated by the relentless silences, were unnerving, but she kept her voice steady.

'I am on holiday. Cary is going to leave his little boy with me when he goes. I only asked because I am trying to help.'

'How can I be sure of you?'

'I am staying at the Scheria. It's easy enough to check. I can show you my passport. Even if you don't remember me, if you have been associated with Cary for a long time you must have met my husband, Tim. Cary's cousin.'

'Ah!' said the man. 'Yes. Tim Johnston. He was killed. You're his widow?'

'Yes. I'll do anything to help. I only want to get the little boy back to England to his mother.'

The dark-haired man, who had been listening in silence, came forward. 'That's a good deal,' he said gruffly. 'We don't want to be stuck with the boy.'

Alix said: 'I've got to get back to my friends before they start looking for me. What are your plans?'

The fair-haired man did not reply. The other man said: 'It's okay, Steve. Don't look

131

a gift horse in the mouth. We don't want the boy. Fix it up here and now.'

'Okay,' he said, as though suddenly making up his mind. 'Where is he? Where's Cary?'

'Up in the hills. In a tiny cottage behind Lakones.'

The second man said: 'Let her do it, Steve. That will save us a day.'

'Could you bring him down tomorrow night?'

'Yes. Yes I could. He's not strong. He had a fever. But I could hire a car.' Her head was spinning with excitement and sheer fright. Underneath, there was a sort of crazy release, a sense of relief that Benjamin was going to be freed from his intolerable situation and returned to England.

'Okay, then. Do that. Bring him here at nine o'clock sharp. Leave the boy in the car. Understand? Don't bring the boy.'

'Yes. I'll do as you say. I want to get back to my friends now. They might come after me.'

There was a weird moment when the three men stood looking at her, clustered together in a half-circle, without speaking. As though, with some diabolical mental telepathy, they were conferring together on a point set above and beyond the conversation. Then the Greek drew his breath in sharply, let it out on a long hiss, and they all relaxed.

'What is your name?' Alix asked. She thought she knew. She thought it was Stephen Scunthorpe, but she was not sure.

'The name of the cruiser is *Venus*,' he replied, and the way he said it told her she had better not ask again for his name. She was suddenly very, very frightened. They were still standing in that closed half-circle with their backs to the Circe, watching her. She side-stepped, and even as she made the move to get away, she had an apprehensive feeling that one of them was going to put out his foot, or his hand. Instead, they melted apart.

She ran like a hare across the dry, uneven ground, tripping, gathering herself together and flying on again, until suddenly she was at the wide-open door of the Circe. She stood there, her heart pounding, her breath dragging, too startled, too shaken even to think while suspicion and fear crowded within her. She wanted to run back through the olive grove to Sabri's and lock herself in her room while she sorted out this new development. But those frightening men would see her go.

Men of good nature, risking their names to help a friend, surely did not behave as they had behaved towards her tonight! Had they come to help Cary? Or had they come to him on some dark business of their own? Cary had inferred there were other people

133

involved in this trouble of his, and that they were to blame. Was that the real reason he was hiding out here? To escape those who would seek to silence his accusations? Or was Cary one of them? He had said Dora had packed in her investigations. Was that because she had found him out?

Torn with anguish, she moved into the taverna and there in front of her was Paul, pushing through the tightly-packed crowd towards her. Alix said in a panic-stricken voice: 'Sorry to be so long. Let's dance.'

Calmly, deliberately, he lifted one hand and picking a leaf from the top of her head, held it out to her. She stared at it, and then laughed feverishly. 'I'm a will o' the wisp, you know that. Come, let's dance.' She pulled him through the crowd and he came willingly enough, but his sombre eyes never left hers while they gyrated to the music.

He had told her she had an expressive face. She hoped to heaven it was not showing the confusion, the panic that was within her now. What might she be doing in bringing Cary down to these men? Was it even conceivable that they had come to find him and dispose of him in order to save their own skins? Or—and this was almost worse—was he guilty? Had Dora found this out, and slipped from the picture? And all the time, at the back of her mind, something was telling her that Benjamin did not fit into any of this story. Benjamin, lost, bored, unwanted by his father, abandoned by his mother...

The music ended on a crash of accordion chords and they went back to the verandah. Paul stood at the rail, smoking. She did not go to join him because she knew what he was doing. He was looking down at the little terrace below where the three yachtsmen would have returned to eat their supper. The Langleys were silent. Jane looked unhappy, Brian pensive. The handbag lay on the table between them. And it was not properly closed! There was a choking sensation in her throat as the muscles contracted from shock. She stared at the double clip, the second one of which had not been pressed down. Out of the side, like a flag, protruded a piece of the white handkerchief in which she had wrapped Cary's passport. Someone had opened her bag!

She lifted her eyes and met theirs, apologetic, curious and somehow, at the same time, showing sympathy. She slid the bag on to her lap. Tomorrow night, Cary would be gone. She would have to tell them the truth when she brought Benjamin to the Scheria. There was nothing to be done now, except keep out of their way. She was making a horrible mess of things because she did not know how to go about being sly and secretive and clever. She was so frightened of this extra passport that it had become an obsession with her so that she never moved an inch without it. And that had proved wrong.

Tomorrow she would disappear with Paul on the caique he had hired, and in the evening she would ask Brian for a loan of his car while he and Jane were at dinner. It would all be over in an hour. Meantime, the night had become a shambles and there was to be no picking up the pieces. She rose. 'I'm going to bed.'

Paul turned. 'I'll take you back.'

They left the Langleys and walked through the olive grove in silence. Paul held her hand. As they crossed the road to Sabri's he said: 'Are you coming out with me in the caique tomorrow?'

'Yes.'

He looked down at her, his face puckered. The moonlight was very bright here, in the open, and she could see his features clearly. 'How can I be sure of that?'

'You can be sure,' she replied. 'What time shall we leave?'

'About ten. Is that too early?'

'No. I'll be ready.'

'I've asked Sabri for two packed lunches.'

'Great.'

Sabri was seated alone at one of the small tables beside the vine. He glanced up, giving them a puzzled look, then his flashing Greek smile. 'You two have been friends now?'

136

'Sabri,' said Paul wearily, 'you and I seem to have got off on the wrong foot.' He pulled out the chair on the other side of the small table and indicated that Alix sit down. 'I'd like to buy you a drink.'

Sabri leaned back in his chair, shouting: 'Nico.' Paul took the other chair. 'Is nice dancing at the Circe?'

'A bit crowded,' Alix told him. 'It's nicer here.'

'Ah!' Sabri was pleased. He looked Alix up and down, appreciatively, and totally without offence. 'You have very pretty dress. Is mimosa.'

'That's very romantic of you,' she replied, laughing. 'Mimosa yellow. What a good colour description.'

Well pleased, he turned to Paul. 'Missus Johnston is very pretty lady.'

'Very,' he agreed gravely. He looked up as Nico appeared. The boy had a newspaper under his arm. 'Is that English?' he asked.

'*Daily Express*, sir. I bring it for you. One of the guests gone to Corfu today.'

'Thanks.' He glanced at the date. 'Today's! They shoot them out fast, now.' He put it down on the table and Alix picked it up, glancing down the front page. It was printed on very flimsy airmail paper and little holes had been rubbed where it was folded. 'What will you have, Alix?'

'Ouzo, please.'

He raised his brows at Sabri, who nodded. 'Three ouzos, Nico.' He turned to Alix. 'Well, is England still afloat?'

She did not answer. She was looking at a paragraph half way down the page and she could not, at that moment, have found a reply because the blood was pounding in her brain and she felt faintly sick. Under the heading: *Financier in Corfu?* she read: *A spokesman for the Light and Heyward Insurance Company, one of the companies who were victims in the alleged swindle involving Cary Johnston, refused to comment on the fact that one of their investigators may have left for Corfu following up a rumour that the financier is hiding there. Johnston speaks fluent Greek and it is thought probable that he has friends on the island.*

*Meantime, the search for Mrs Dora Johnston and their son Benjamin has been stepped up following enquiries from her relations who are worried by a report that Johnston left the country alone.*

She looked up, her eyes dilating, her mouth dry. Sabri and Paul were talking about the weather.

'North is okay,' Sabri was saying. 'Strong south westerly ... It not much ... yet.'

Nico was coming with a little tray and the three tiny glasses side-by-side with three tumblers of water. She heard Paul say: '... hope not.' Her hearing was clicking on and

138

off, as though she was stunned, or ill. Paul was taking some money out of his pocket. He tossed a packet of cigarettes on the table. Alix, scarcely realizing what she was doing, reached out and took one.

Paul laughed. 'Good lord! You, smoking! You're one long surprise.' He flicked a lighter and she inhaled. She had not smoked since Tim died.

She looked at Paul steadily. She was thinking of him sitting patiently at the look-out this afternoon like a cat waiting for a mouse. She wondered if Paul really had booked a caique, or if that was a red herring. And she thought with some bitterness of the way he had picked her up on the plane and joined her at Sabri's, pretending to be in love.

## CHAPTER THIRTEEN

Alix dozed fitfully. At sun-up she would set out for Lakones. To warn Cary of Paul. To acquaint him of Stephen Scunthorpe's appearance. To ask her own questions, and, if necessary, to spirit Benjamin away.

Sabri's was eerily silent in the early dawn. Alix tiptoed along the narrow passage, then down the steps. For the first time since her arrival a wind was blowing, stirring up little eddies of dust at the side of the road. She looked longingly at the Langleys' hired car and wished she had hired one herself. It was going to take her more than an hour to walk to the village. So early in the morning, there was little chance of picking up a lift.

She set out up the steep, silent, winding road, powdered with early morning mist, walking fast where it levelled out, cutting across a hair-pin where the terrain of the ground allowed. Though the looming mountain still held the sun in the low east it was surprisingly hot for there was no breeze here where the road was tucked tightly between sheltering woods.

By the time she reached Lakones the village was beginning to stir. Somewhere a clock struck the hour and there was a little peal of bells. Alix went through the village and set off down the road towards Cary's tiny house. As she went by the little green dwelling with the scarlet door a man emerged and looked at her curiously, said something in Greek, then flexing his muscles, went to a bucket standing on the ground and began to wash his face and arms. Two little donkeys dozed contentedly on the edge of the lemon grove beside the house.

Cary's place was silent, the one window shuttered, the door closed. Alix knocked, waited. She then tried the door. It was locked. She went round to the bedroom window and called softly: 'Cary, it's Alix.'

The curtain moved fractionally and Cary's face was faintly visible behind the dusty glass. She returned to the front to wait and several moments later the door opened. Cary had pulled on a pair of shorts and a shirt. His dark hair was tousled and he was rubbing the sleep from his eyes. 'What the devil are you doing here at this hour?'

Alix stepped inside. 'I have come with news, good and bad.'

He looked at her sharply. 'Give me the bad first.'

'There is a man at the Scheria, a Paul Crispin, who is looking for you. The Light and Heyward Insurance Company sent him. And I am afraid he knows where you are.'

Cary did not, as she expected, look surprised but his face hardened and he gripped her arms with fingers that hurt. 'How did he find out where I am?'

'Unfortunately, he wanted to swim with me yesterday afternoon and I had no excuse not to. I couldn't get rid of him so I pretended to have a siesta, then I scarpered. He came up to the look-out.'

'Looking for you? Why the look-out?' Cary's voice was sharp with suspicion.

'I dare say he looked on the beach first. He probably walked up through the olive groves when he didn't find me there, and came out in Lakones.' She knew Paul had come by car, but she had to allay Cary's totally irrelevant suspicions. 'He saw me come up the road into the square. That's why I said he knows where you are. If he is looking for you, and the paper says he is, and he suspects me of being in touch, then he is going to check on the places I go to.'

'The paper!' Cary barked.

'I am sorry. I should have said that first. You're confusing me. Cary, why are you treating me like this?' Like an enemy, she might have added.

As though he had not heard her protest, he said in a cold, waiting voice: 'What was in the paper?'

'Someone from the Scheria was in Corfu yesterday and brought back an *Express*. It said there were rumours you were here and that Paul had come to investigate.'

Cary looked down at her queerly. 'Is that all it said?'

'Cary, please let me go. You're hurting terribly.'

'Keep your voice down. You'll wake the boy. Tell me what was in the paper.' His fingers relaxed a little, but he did not let her go.

She told him, as far as she could remember. He did not take his eyes from her face. 'You're obviously friendly with this fellow. Paul.' He said the name very deliberately.

142

'Cary, please let go of me. You're frightening me. I haven't done anything wrong. I am here to help you.'

Reluctantly, his hands dropped to his sides. 'What's it all about?' he asked. 'What are you so flustered about?'

Not flustered, but certainly upset. She had been so nearly in love.

'I think now he may have followed me here, to Corfu. It is possible. He spoke to me on the plane. I thought he was just trying to pick me up. He may have been checking on all your relatives. He may have thought I would lead him to you.' The bitterness, the hurt, the disappointment, came through like a shaft.

'You've been a great help, haven't you!' said Cary savagely.

She was shaken by his anger, but she managed to control her own. 'Yes,' she said, deliberately misunderstanding him. 'I have done my best to help. But if you don't want me any more, say so. I have your passport here in my bag. You shall have it back now.' She swung her bag forward. 'I can't think why you should react like this. Paul is not the police. He is only an insurance investigator. He can't arrest you.'

For a full moment Cary did not answer. When she could not stand the silence any longer she said: 'There was something else in the paper. Dora's family is worried about

143

her.'

'She'll be in touch, now she's dropped me.'

'The paper said you left the country alone. How would they know that?'

'They don't know, do they? I left with the boy. You've seen his name on the passport.'

'Yes. But the article said they were worried about Dora and Benjamin.' He was silent. 'I've something else to tell you, Cary. Some men have come in on a motor cruiser. Stephen—I think—Scunthorpe, and two others.'

He jumped. 'Steve! Steve's here! God Damn! Why didn't you say so?'

'Because you asked for the bad news first. Is this good news? Is he the man you've been waiting for?'

'You're damned right,' said Cary. All the anger, the tension, the fear seemed to drop away from him.

'How did you come across them?'

She told him about recognizing the man Scunthorpe and he gave her that odd, narrow look again. 'You've got a mighty good memory, haven't you? You only met him once, more than two years ago.'

'I've a good memory for faces. And besides, he has a distinctive birthmark.' She did not add that some of the people at the party at Richmond Hill had impressed themselves indelibly on her. They were a part of the unattractive picture in her mind when she talked Tim out of joining Cary and Dora for that Corfu holiday. The decision that had been so disastrous for Tim. 'They have come to take you away. I am to get you down to the yacht basin at nine tonight.'

The anger had gone right out of him. 'Thank God for that.' He suddenly looked weak and spent. He sat with shoulders slumped and head drooped forward. She stood looking at him unhappily, torn, suspicious, worried. She opened her shoulder bag and took the passport out. 'I won't need this any more.'

He looked up, lifting a hand to stop her. 'I want you to go into Corfu and see if there is any more mail.'

She did not want to go. She did not want to help him any more. If he was hand in glove with those strange, menacing men who had spoken to her last night, then she could no longer believe in his total innocence. 'I don't know if I can,' she said.

He stared at her, his eyes narrowing. 'What, exactly, do you mean?' he enquired, his voice cold, suspicious again.

'I've arranged to go out on a caique with Paul Crispin for an all-day picnic.' It was not the moment to say she had suspected, after reading the newspaper, that the caique might be a red herring. She had to think around that, now these suspicions of Cary were

145

flooding her mind. Might not Paul turn the tables on her today? Having established the fact that he was using her to find Cary, it was easy enough to see that he might well ditch her today and come up here. Yet, he had seemed genuinely anxious last night that they should spend the day alone.

'You're going out with the chap who is after me!' Cary spoke slowly, incredulously.

'While he is out with me he can't come after you.'

'Is that why you're going?'

'For heaven's sake,' she flared, unnerved, 'I am trying to help you. It must be pretty obvious. And anyway, why should you care if Paul finds you now? You're going tonight! Of course the only sensible thing is for me to spend all day with him.'

'No,' Cary said, speaking softly but still with that strange, steely look in his eyes. 'No. You had better come with me.'

'Where to?' She was suddenly alarmed.

'I'd suggest Castel Angelo.'

'Castel Angelo! It's miles away. You'd never get there unless you've made a simply miraculous recovery since yesterday.'

'I haven't done that. You'll have to get me transport.'

'There's no road to Castel Angelo.' Sabri had mentioned that.

'You'll have to hire a donkey. There are a couple of them at the little place up the

146

track. You've said your friend Paul knows where I am. If he comes here and sees me, he can go straight to the police. And I am a sitting duck until nine o'clock.'

'What could they do, without a warrant for your arrest?' She forced herself to look at him steadily and he looked back at her, examining the suspicion, the hostility behind her eyes. She knew it was there, but she could not hide it. Cary was guilty of something, there was now no doubt in her mind. She wanted to walk out and leave him to it, but there was little Benjamin in the next room.

Weirdly, he seemed to read her thoughts. He said: 'If you want me to leave the boy with you, you had better do as I say.'

'Otherwise?'

'I can easily take him with me.'

'To North Africa? If he doesn't like Greek food, how do you think he'll fare there?'

'If children survive the flies and bugs to Benjamin's age, they're usually all right. But an English boy—'

'This is blackmail!'

'Don't raise your voice. You'll wake the child. He is going to need all the sleep he can get. He needs strength for where he is going.'

'You bastard!'

When he spoke he did so slowly, still deliberately, but with a certain crushed warmth. 'Blood is thicker than water, Alix.

You owe something to the Johnston family. You murdered Tim, after all, didn't you?'

Tears sprang to her eyes. It was one thing to blame oneself, to torture oneself with doubt. It was quite another for Cary to look at her with Tim's eyes, as hostile as Tim's had been when he said: 'Okay, I'll go to bloody Yorkshire with you if you're so bloody sure it's right.' Alix crumpled. Everything that had happened over the past two years, everything that had occurred here on Corfu, the fear, the strain, the worry, the doubt and self-doubt. The growing panic about Benjamin's safety, the fears of, and for, Cary. They all swept over her in an enveloping wave.

She felt Cary's arm go round her and pull her to him. She put her face down on his shoulder and wept. 'We're a family,' he said. 'We've got to stick together. Nobody's perfect.'


## CHAPTER FOURTEEN

She went back down the track to the house where she had seen the little donkeys in the lemon grove. She was carrying a note from Cary, written in Greek, asking if she could hire the two animals for the day. Her mind was working traitorously on how she could get Benjamin away. With the child in her custody, she could send a message to the *Venus* telling his friends where to find Cary. One of the men from the Circe would no doubt be willing to row out to them with a letter. Then she would go into hiding in Corfu until she had seen the Consul and arranged to take Benjamin home. Whatever Cary had done, it was not her affair, and she wanted no part of it. Only the child was her responsibility, and somehow she had to get him out of here.

The little donkeys, saddled with their empty pannier bags, were already tied up at the fence, apparently ready for the day's work. Without help, Cary would never make Castel Angelo. A wild idea flew through her mind. She would race down to Paleocastritsa and get Paul to come up. But what could he do? Even if he was willing to be a party to abducting Cary's son, Cary was an unknown quantity and she had no right to involve Paul in possible danger.

It had seemed, in the beginning, that the Greeks were sheltering him. Did their assistance merely add up to the turning of a blind eye? Madame Vassilakis, it was true, supplied meals and had unhesitatingly called a doctor, but she spent no time at the little house and Cary's odd, belligerent, nervy manner was indicative of a man who was putting in too much time on his own. If Cary had friends here, as the newspaper had intimated, where were they?

The Greek came out of the tiny green house to stare at her. She went up the short path and handed him the letter. He read it and shook his head. Cary had told her to wave the drachmas under his nose. No Greek could resist money, he said. She took out the notes and held them up. The man grinned. 'Okay. Okay.' He pocketed the money and led her over to the fence where the donkeys were tethered. He undid the ropes, then turning to her said something earnestly in Greek which she did not understand.

She led the little donkeys along the track to the house. Cary was standing in the doorway. He relaxed when he saw her. 'You're a pretty big man for these little fellows,' Alix said as she came up to the broken fence and set about tethering them. Cary went back inside without answering. Benjamin met her at the door wearing a pair of jeans she had washed yesterday, and the red shirt. He was eating cereal out of a bowl. When he saw the donkeys he gave a little shriek of delight. 'Can I have a ride?'

'But of course. That's what I brought them for. We're going on a picnic in the hills. But first of all, I think I'll brush your hair. It looks like a mat.'

Benjamin dashed one hand across his hair

and gave her a twinkling, engaging smile.

She followed Cary into the kitchen. 'Have you collected up the food for lunch?'

'I've taken it all,' he replied, pushing Benjamin's cornflakes into the top of a canvas bag. 'You never know. We can't come back here.'

She put a hand on his arm. 'What do you mean when you say "you never know"?'

'Perhaps I should say I never know. It's entirely up to you, and you've proved something of an unknown quantity, haven't you, cousin Alix?'

She turned away. 'As you said,' she retorted cryptically, 'we're a family. We ought to stick together.' But she kept her head carefully averted as she spoke.

*　　*　　*

Cary looked enormous on the tiny donkey with his feet hanging barely a foot from the track.

'Are you sure you're not too heavy?'

'You should see what they carry. They virtually disappear under some of their loads.'

'Poor things. They're truly named as beasts of burden. Now, Benjamin, you and the food for this one.' Cary said he had hidden the suitcase in some bushes well away from the house. It did not tie in with his remark that they would not be returning here, but Alix was past caring. She lifted Benjamin on to the donkey's back and took the rope lead in her hand. The sun was rising higher in the sky. The track that led away into the hills was stony and narrow, set by the pattering hooves of goats and donkeys. Here it meandered between great beds of green myrtle and tall heather.

Benjamin, excited about the journey, chattered happily. 'What is my donkey's name, Alix?'

'Shall we call him—sorry, her—Aphrodite?'

'Aphrodite!' The little boy pronounced the name with difficulty. 'I never heard that name before.'

'It's Greek. Aphrodite was a goddess.'

'What's a goddess?'

'Er—an important lady who lived in the sky.'

Benjamin looked up at the gentian blue arc above them. 'What did she do there?'

'She made flowers spring up out of the ground.'

'Gosh. I don't think my donkey could do that.'

She heard Cary's husky laugh and a little of the tenseness went. 'Haven't you noticed the flowers by the side of the track? Irises, and wild roses, and poppies?'

'I don't fink my donkey got them up.'

'Maybe not. But everywhere Aphrodite went sparrows and doves flew about her and I've seen a lot of sparrows, haven't you, since we set out? And several doves.'

Benjamin was enchanted. 'Yes, I have. What shall we call Daddy's donkey?'

'Let's call him Heracles,' she suggested, stepping back as the track widened to walk with one hand on the little animal's neck. 'Heracles was given twelve tasks...'

With his donkey pattering along the track, Benjamin settled down contentedly to hear the twelve tasks of Heracles.

They went down a long slope then rose, and over the brow of the next hill there were olive groves, lifted on their terraces, silvery in the morning sun. Steep little hillsides where black-clad peasants worked, bent double, over vines. A shepherd driving his goats.

The hills were silent except for Alix's voice telling Benjamin the Greek fables. Pandora's box. The Lion and the Mouse. The Fox and the Woodcutter. She drew his attention to the tinkle of the sheep bell, the distant bark of a shepherd's dog, to shoals of butterflies fluttering over bushes like coloured snowflakes on a lifting wind.

Benjamin's unkempt, little-boy-lost look had fled. His chin was high, his cheeks flushed, his blond hair scattered by the breeze. 'If I had a camera I'd make a Christmas card out of you,' she told him.

153

Benjamin wriggled coyly. 'I'm not a Christmas card. I'm a boy.'

A boy whom nobody wants, Alix thought again. It seemed incredible that Dora, opting out of her husband's affairs, should not come to collect her child. Was this what their journey to Castel Angelo was really about? She had been unable to find an acceptable reason for Cary's running away from Paul. Was he, in fact, afraid that Dora might turn up and collect the child? In which case, he did intend to break his promise to her and take Benjamin away in the yacht. But why? He made no secret of the fact that the child was a nuisance to him. Somehow, she had to get him away.

They had been walking for an hour when Cary called Alix to stop. He slid one foot to the ground and swung the other over. 'There's Castel Angelo in front now.' A tiny white square of a building on an enormously high peak still some distance away. Shading her eyes, Alix looked across bush and mountain top and her spirits quailed. 'There must be an easier way to get to it than this.'

'Of course. There's a road that goes a certain distance, but do you want people to see us?'

'No, of course not.'

'I'll show you a short way to get back. It won't take too long.' Cary assured her placatingly. 'Here, you get on Heracles,' he

154

offered gruffly.

She was hot, and she was also a little footsore. Apart from the brief argumentative respite at the little house, she had been walking since daybreak. She flopped down on the sun-bleached grass at the side of the track. 'I am all right. My choice of sandals was rather unfortunate. The stones seem to go right through this leather.'

'Come on, then. Have a ride.' Cary, now that they were safely in the hills, seemed infinitely more relaxed. His voice was almost gentle.

She stretched out on the slope, arms above her head. 'I'll be okay. The doctor said you were to rest and sitting on a donkey isn't exactly resting. Besides, you've got the journey back tonight.'

But Cary insisted. He wanted to get on, he said. Alix must have her rest on the donkey. 'Don't think I'm not grateful,' he said unexpectedly. 'You've been very good to us, and I do appreciate it. If I was tough with you it's because I'm not myself. I'll make it up to you, some time.'

She slid one jean-clad leg over the little donkey's back and settled herself on his rump the way the peasants sat, then looking up at Cary, her eyes steady, she said: 'All I ask is that you keep your promise for tonight.'

'I'll do that, if you keep yours.'

155

That she was not going to be able to keep it was another matter. He could have guessed then, and possibly did, but there was no way Alix could know what Fate held in store.

## CHAPTER FIFTEEN

Considering Michael the Despot had built the castle in the year 1214, Alix thought soberly, broken walls and stone blocks were about all one could expect to find now. Cary, she had to believe, had come here for the pure and simple reason that the ruin was easily pin-pointable, hard to get at, a safe shelter for a day and, for all she knew, had the advantage, though high above, of at least being near to the sea.

There was a tiny chapel (not a relic from the 13th century but something the Greeks had put up comparatively recently) of brick and plaster, similar to those one saw dotted around the island. The view was spell-binding. Mile after mile of blue water stretching westward to an indefinite horizon where it merged palely with the sky's rim. Nearer the land, a wind had whipped up little trimmings of foam. There were no ships, no fishing caiques, no sign of life. It was like being on top of the world from which the people had gone.

As Alix stood on a rock looking down the immense drop to the frothy, rock-broken sea below a sharp wind cut in unexpectedly, filling her damp shirt, tossing her hair. Inland, the hills rolled away, mile after mile of steeply terraced vineyards, cypress trees like tall, lonely sentinels, rocky outcrops and one thin, torn ribbon of road.

It was nearly mid-day. Apart from a quick drink at a mountain stream, nothing had passed her lips since the ouzo she and Paul had shared with Sabri at midnight. She went back to the little chapel. Cary and Benjamin were emerging hand-in-hand. It crossed Alix's mind that this was the first time she had seen Cary show any sign of affection for the boy, and as suddenly, she realized what was behind it. Cary was waiting for her to leave, and he would hold Benjamin in an iron grip until she did. Well, she thought resignedly, she should have known, and perhaps it was her own fault for giving too much away. She would have to carry out Cary's orders and wait until tonight.

Pretending she had not noticed anything, she went into the chapel. A tiled floor, icons, lamps, a little can of oil and some ancient and rather dusty candles.

'It's shelter if you should need it,' she commented as she emerged.

'I am hungry,' announced Benjamin. 'Can

we have the picnic now?' He pointed to the lumps protruding from Aphrodite's pannier bag. Cary had hobbled the little donkeys and they were nibbling at the thin, dry grass.

'You're not the only one,' said Alix. 'Heavens! That sun is hot! Thank goodness for this lovely wind.' Cary released Benjamin and swung round sharply. He raised a hand, frowning, then went over to where the ground dropped away, almost sheer for hundreds of feet. He stared in silence down towards Paleocastritsa, then turned slowly and gazed out to sea. Alix watched his every move, but when he returned, looking worried, he again gripped Benjamin's hand.

'What's the matter, Cary?'

'Nothing. Look here, hadn't you better get going? It's a hell of a long way back, and don't forget you have to get in to the Corfu post office.'

'Without anything to eat?' Alix flared. She was hot, tired and worried. Her nerves were sawn ragged with trying to think of a way to take Benjamin, and now there was the disappointment of knowing it was not going to be possible.

The little boy looked up. He saw her flushed cheeks, her flashing eyes. 'What's the matter?' he quavered. 'Isn't there any lunch?'

'Of course, my darling. Of course. There's lots of lunch and we're going to have it now.'

She turned to Cary and keeping her voice

158

pleasant for Benjamin's sake, she said: 'You know, I have been up since daybreak.'

He only replied: 'You could have had some breakfast at the house.'

In his turn, he stood watching her while she emptied the pannier and put the food on the chapel floor. Outside, the beating sun was everywhere, casting no more than a few inches of shadow from the walls, but the wind was dancing in over the cliff top, taking the sting out of it.

As she went backwards and forwards, Alix saw Benjamin make a half-hearted effort to release himself, but Cary did not relax his grip and the child stayed. It was as though this surprising sign of affection had touched his lonely heart and he accepted with gratitude.

When the food was ready she lifted the pannier bags down from the donkeys' backs and dropped them by the chapel wall. As she turned to go inside she saw a corner of tweed and realizing it must be Cary's jacket, lifted it out and gave it a shake. A hard, metal object cracked against her wrist and thinking one of the tins had somehow found its way into Cary's pocket, she reached in. Her fingers closed round something that was certainly not a tin of food. She drew it out, her eyes dilating, her blood freezing in her veins. A gun!

She started and nearly dropped it as Cary,

close behind her, said: 'What are you doing, Cousin Alix?'

She swung round, white-faced. 'Cary!'

He came right up to her. 'What a meddlesome girl you are, to be sure!'

'Cary! Why have you got a gun?'

He took it from her, gently but firmly, his eyes never leaving her face. 'Every Greek carries a gun. And a knife,' he added.

She passed her tongue over dry lips. Of course foreigners carried guns. It was different for them. When an Englishman carried one he did it for a purpose. 'Why did you bring it?'

'To shoot game, of course.'

'With a revolver?'

They stared at each other for a long time in silence. At last Cary said: 'I told you there is a lot you don't know about me. I've had a deal to do with the political uprisings in Greece.'

'Why? What have Greece's politics to do with you?'

'The provision of arms for insurgents is a very profitable business.'

She said with disgust: 'Is that why you're on your own here? Why Madame Vassilakis merely provides food—because she's scared not to—and no one else comes near?'

'Could be.' He put the gun back in the pocket of his jacket and covered it with the bag. 'Come inside,' he said as though

160

nothing at all had happened. 'The boy has already started lunch.'

Benjamin was seated on the floor with a chicken leg in his fingers. For his sake, she had to pretend nothing had happened. Cary had cut up the remains of the chicken. She took a piece, though she scarcely knew how she would swallow it. 'If you're going tonight,' she said, 'then it's all over. Why do you want me to go to the post office again?'

'I am waiting for a very important message. I don't want to go until I get it.'

'So what will you do if it has not come tonight?'

'Re-think,' Cary replied tersely. He eyed her narrowly. 'What do these questions mean? That you're not so anxious to help me, now?'

'You know how I feel,' she replied, keeping her voice light and smiling down at Benjamin though her stomach was a knot of anger and her face felt as though it would split in two. 'How were you going to get your post if I had not turned up?'

'I'd have got a Greek to do it.' Cary had said they would do anything for money, and certainly her experience with the donkeys had proved him right.

'Who was that other letter from?' He had lied first of all, saying it came from Dora, then later told her Dora had opted out.

'I am setting up a business,' he said. 'I

can't live on fresh air.'

'Arms?' He did not answer. She said carefully, examining her chicken wing with total absorption: 'The papers said you got away with a lot of money.'

'If they don't get news, they make it up, don't they?'

'I don't know.'

'Well, I'm telling you.'

'Where are you setting up this business? You said you were going to North Africa.'

'You ask a lot of questions, don't you?'

'I am involved. I think you owe me more of an explanation than you've given.' When he did not answer she went on: 'These men, Scunthorpe, and the other one and the Greek—are they going into business with you?' She noticed that he did not volunteer the other man's name.

'Nothing is settled,' he replied evasively. 'That's why it is so important for me to get this message.'

'Will the message tell you where to go?'

'The message is private,' he said with heavy finality. 'You've been very good and I'd be glad if you would just go for the message and stay out of my affairs.'

'You're not expecting to get back to England for a long time, are you Cary?' She did not look at him as she said it.

He hesitated. 'With Dora not involved now, it is going to be slower, isn't it?'

162

'Who will do the digging for information to clear you now?' She no longer believed that story about his staying out of the way while Dora assembled proof that would clear him. 'Not Scunthorpe.'

'He's helping in a different way, isn't he?' He did not like her questions. He sounded edgy. 'I have many friends, Alix.'

'Yes. I am sure you have.' She paused a moment.

'Cary, tell me why Dora opted out.'

'She had lost faith in the possibility of clearing me and she didn't want to be tied to a sinking ship.'

'Is that what the letter said? The letter I brought?'

'Yes.'

'Then why, do you suppose, she has not come out to collect Benjamin?'

'How could she? The police would follow her. She'd know I would send the boy home when I could.'

'That newspaper said Dora's parents were worried about her.'

'I dare say they have been. She promised not to get in touch until I got clear away. When I am safely in North Africa I'll send word and she can relax.'

'I don't understand.'

'She'll be cross-questioned when she appears, won't she? The police are pretty adept at tripping people up. She won't take the risk until I am safe.'

For a wife who had let her husband down, Dora Johnston sounded inexplicably loyal.

## CHAPTER SIXTEEN

Of course there had never been any chance of getting Benjamin away, Alix thought, as she clambered down the steep path that wound by steps and often near-vertical gradients among the ruined remains of the old castle walls. The child would have been slow, and if she had to carry him she would have been slower still. Even in his weakened state, Cary could have caught them if he so wished. Benjamin was a hostage against her returning with his precious message. That message must be mighty important, she thought. She had said: 'It is a very long way up here. You say there is a road beyond that olive grove down there, about forty minutes' walk away. Why don't you and Benjamin meet me there tonight? There is no need for me to come all the way.'

'Be there at eight o'clock. Will you be able to bring a car?'

She had thought of borrowing the Langleys' car, but in the light of what she now knew about Cary, she did not want to involve them. She said: 'I'll go into Corfu on

164

a bus, hire a car and drive back. But what will happen to Aphrodite and Heracles?'

'Someone will find them,' Cary replied casually.

'Cary!'

'What the hell!'

In the end, she had asked him to bring the donkeys down to the road and leave them on a terrace beneath the olive trees. She could come back in the morning and return them to their owner.

It was unbearably hot here again, with the sea wind cut off by the mountain spur. As she descended the steep slope among the cypresses, the ilex, the bracken and the trailing brambles, Alix tried to tell herself that Cary's black business dealings were none of her affair. Her business was the returning of Benjamin unharmed to his mother. But Cary lied too easily. She could not really trust him to leave Benjamin with her. And yet, not trusting him, what could she do about it? The Langleys? Paul? No one in their right senses would set out to take a child from his father. More especially from a father who had a gun. No, she had a choice of two decisions. To go ahead as she had agreed, and trust Cary to keep his word, bearing in mind that once she realized he was not going to keep his word it would be too late. Or, she could take it upon herself to telephone Dora.

There was something very strange about the whole situation with regard to Cary's wife. None of what Cary had said about her made sense. One day she had been in disguise busying herself with the job of proving Cary's innocence. The next, she had dropped him. It followed, since she had not been in touch, that she had also dropped her little boy. Yet Alix found this hard to accept. She wondered if one could put a call through from a foreign country when one was not in possession of the telephone number. If Dora had stopped her investigations with regard to Cary's affairs, Alix assumed she would return home. The police would not hold her responsible for her husband's misdeeds.

Following the narrow track through bramble and waist-high parsley, past olives silvered in the sun and echoing with cicadas, Alix came at last upon the road that snaked through the hills north of Lakones. There were flat terraces here where olives grew. They had crossed this road, she was certain, on the way up. Cary had said it was not too far from here to the village.

Half an hour's walk later, hot, footsore and weary, she saw the beginnings of the village. She came up to the look-out with nerves strung tight, half expecting Paul to be there, but there was no one. And no bus. A wind such as she had felt on Castel Angelo danced in and out of the tree tops, swinging the tips of the tall cypresses and sending little eddies of dust swirling across the square. She held her shirt away from her body and ran her fingers through her hair, tossing the strands in the wind.

Her feet were very sore now and a blister had come up on the ball of her left foot. An old woman, driving a little flock of goats through an arch between two buildings, gave her a curious stare. Black-haired, black-browed men playing cards in front of a house with broken shutters eyed her with interest but did not speak.

Here, the retaining wall was broken above the steeply-shelving olive grove. Even picking her way carefully she was bound to reach the bay more quickly by taking the short cut. She clambered over the broken stones and slid down the shale.

When she broke clear of the woodland and groves the wind came beating in and she saw that the umbrellas on the beach had been taken down. Sabri was standing hands on hips in the office doorway, scowling. He saw her and his face lit up. 'Ah! Missus Johnston! You have been walked long way. You have good exercise?'

'I'm afraid I rather overdid my walk today, Sabri. And now, I have to go into Corfu. When is the next bus?'

'One hour, perhaps.'

'What about a taxi?'

'Taxis come dinner time, bring guests. Is too early.'

'Well—an hour. I think I'll have a swim.'

Sabri shook his head. 'Is not nice in the water. All the sand stir up, and cold water come in from bottom of sea. Cold and dirt,' Sabri told her quaintly. He raised one arm to the heavens. 'Is strong south westerly blowing.'

'Ah well, it will have to be a shower.' She turned to go, then swung back again. 'How long does a south westerly blow?'

His brown face creased into a hundred different lines, his shoulders rose and his hands came out in supplication. 'Is up to Saint Spiridon. One day, two day, three day. Is bad now.' He shook his head gravely. 'This morning the yachts rush out to sea. You hear them, Missus Johnston? They make peep-peep-peep in the dark.'

She said in a horrified rush: 'Why did they go?' knowing the answer.

'Here, they get dash on rocks,' Sabri explained. 'Sm-ash! They ride wind out at sea and come in again when north wind come. Maybe tomorrow. Maybe four, five days.'

She stared at him. She could not take it in, at first, the fact that Cary and Benjamin were holed up at Castel Angelo in a tiny chapel and might be there for four or five days. That she was not going to be able to get Benjamin

168

out of this awful situation. That she was tied by blackmail to this man whom she was convinced now was a criminal. Whom she did not want to help.

The horror of the situation welled up in her slowly as the shock ebbed away. 'Oh God!' she said, holding a hand to her eyes.

'Something is matter, Missus Johnston?' Sabri enquired solicitously.

'No. Oh no. Sabri, if a taxi should happen to come down, please stop it for me.'

'Yes, Missus Johnston. I do.'

She went blindly up the stairs at the side of the hotel and along to her room.

## CHAPTER SEVENTEEN

'Barrington?' echoed Lucilla Godfrey in astonishment. 'I don't know anyone called Barrington.'

'He says it's about your niece.'

'Ah-h!'

'The point is, you must keep that lamp on your foot for forty minutes and I've another patient due as soon as you've finished, so I can't let you go out to him, unless you want to miss your treatment. I really cannot over-run. It's not fair to the people who come after you.' She was the old-fashioned type of nurse, stiffly starched, terrifyingly clean. 'He says he wants to see you urgently. I could let him in. It's up to you.'

Lucilla heaved an enormous sigh. She looked down critically at the rumpled stocking lying on the floor. At the white leg, with its puffed ankle. There was not much she would not do for Alix, but really ... The man had a nerve, demanding to see her like this. 'You'd think he might wait forty minutes,' she grumbled.

'I don't know, Mrs Godfrey, but I wouldn't be surprised if he was from the police.'

'The police?' Lucilla went rigid.

The nurse lowered her voice: 'He's got that air about him. Is there anything wrong?'

'Nothing specific, that I know of.' But dread was creeping over her like an incoming tide.

He was a tall, thin-faced man with a quick manner and alert eyes. In one split second he took in the bare walls, the hard narrow couch, the machine in the corner, the functional cupboard and herself. 'Mrs Godfrey,' he said without preamble. 'I am very sorry to intrude on you like this. I would not have done it if—'

She silenced him brusquely. 'All right, young man, you've done it and I assume you had good reason. Nothing has happened to my niece, I hope?'

'No, no.'

'Then who are you?'

'I am making some enquiries with regard to Cary Johnston, the missing financier. I have had a call from Corfu asking me to investigate a Mrs Alix Johnston.'

Now that Alix was safe and well she was outraged. 'Who is investigating my niece?'

'We simply want to eliminate her, that's all. We want to know who she is.'

'Ah!' said Lucilla shrewdly. 'She's in Corfu, the notorious Cary's stamping ground! Well, I can tell you, young man, that she is there on an innocent holiday. And I should be with her.'

'Yes. That's how I traced you. Through a cancelled ticket. I got your address from Olympic Airways.'

'Yorkshire?'

'Someone at your home—a neighbour, she said she was looking after the place—gave me the name of your hotel and the receptionist gave me the name of the clinic.'

'Sleuth!' said Lucilla enigmatically, looking down at her ankle and wishing the wretched man did not have her at such a disadvantage. There was nothing very sophisticated about an exposed seventy-year-old leg. Now that her fears with regard to Alix had been put to rest, she was illogically angry with herself for letting him in. 'So! Has Cary Johnston been run to ground on Corfu?'

'We're not sure. What relation is your niece to him, Mrs Godfrey? I gather from the way you spoke that she is related.'

'She had the misfortune,' replied Lucilla cryptically, 'to marry Cary's cousin. But if you're thinking that she is in Corfu to contact Cary, then think again, young man. For one thing, she scarcely knew him and far from admiring him, she tried to keep her husband and Cary apart.'

'Why?'

'Because, to put it bluntly, Tim had Cary's penchant for throwing money around without Cary's ability to earn it. So you think Cary is on Corfu? I should have thought that was the last place he would go, if only because it's where people would look first. He was always dashing off there on business or pleasure.'

Barrington pushed his hands into his pockets and went to lean, cross-legged, against the cupboard, looking down at her. 'On the other hand, he knows the island. A man who wants to keep out of sight is at a tremendous advantage if he is acquainted with the country and the people. Besides, as you say, it is known he had business interests there. He may have had to go back.'

'Yes, and what were his business interests?' Lucilla gave the man a penetrating look.

'Your niece didn't know?'

'She suspected it was something fishy. Was it?'

'Fishy? We-ll, it was straightforward arms dealing. He ran guns across the Mediterranean to the Arab countries. He is thought to be behind some of those anarchist groups that are springing up in Jordan. And before that he had a good deal to do with the Greek junta. That's why it is possible he is hiding somewhere in Greece—and more especially Corfu—because he is known, and feared, there. The Greeks might not want him, but they could be nervous of crossing him. He'd get co-operation in Corfu, if he paid for it.'

'What has all this to do with my niece?'

'It's thought she might have gone out to help him. What I really needed to establish from you is whether your niece is, in fact, his wife travelling under a false passport. You have already answered that. The fact remains that Dora Johnston and the child are missing.'

'I should think they're with him. And I can tell you, quite categorically, that my niece has not gone out to help Cary. She has gone because I insisted, for private and personal reasons, that she go. I was to go with her. And then, most unfortunately, this old injury played me up and the doctor insisted that I should have immediate treatment.'

'What sort of person is your niece, Mrs

Godfrey?'

'She is honest. She would be very unsympathetic with someone who was trafficking in lives.' Lucilla looked up at Barrington through narrowed eyes. 'That's what arms dealing is about, isn't it?'

'I didn't exactly mean that. Is she kind? Soft?'

'Kind, yes. Soft, no. Why do you ask?'

'In the hypothetical situation that she should, in spite of your reassurances to the contrary, have known Cary Johnston was on Corfu—'

'She *did not know*, young man.'

'How could you be sure?' His insistence was quiet, a practised art.

'Because I know my niece.'

'Then let me put it this way. If she should discover, on arrival, that he was there—'

'It's too much of a coincidence, isn't it?' Lucilla retorted sharply.

'No, I don't think so. Someone at her hotel might be in touch with Johnston. If she should discover he was there, do you think she would help him?'

'I don't think she would want to,' returned Lucilla, deeply worried now. 'But yes, since you put it that way, I don't think she would turn her back on anyone who was in trouble, whether she was related or not. And now, young man, what are you going to do with this information I have given you?'

'Add it to the dossier. You have helped us a good deal, Mrs Godfrey. There is a man in Corfu who is watching your niece. I'll telegraph him.'

'That she is a red herring?'

'More precisely, that she is not Dora Johnston.'

Lucilla nodded. She did not like his evasive reply at all. 'Is a warrant out for Cary's arrest?'

'Not yet. I am sorry to have disturbed you in this way. It was a complicated process, running you to ground. The matter was becoming rather urgent.'

The nurse came back into the room. 'I saw him go. Is everything all right, Mrs Godfrey?'

'No, my dear, it isn't. It isn't all right at all. I've a good mind to get on a plane and go to Greece.'

'Your doctor wouldn't like that at all.'

'It's a matter of priorities, isn't it?'

'If you value your mobility you will take your doctor's advice.'

'I value it all right,' Lucilla retorted, 'but I'm a tough old Yorkshire woman, my dear, and I can stand up to a good deal.'

'You're not as young as you used to be,' the nurse observed tritely. 'You would be well advised to think about that ankle.'

Heavens! Had she thought about much else for the past fortnight? Thumping around on a stick, it was not lightly put out of her mind. Without deciding anything, it would not hurt to ring Olympic Airways and see if there was a vacant seat on a Corfu-bound plane.

*    *    *

Paul was starting his car when Sabri came running across the road. 'Mister Crispin, you are going to Corfu?'

'Yes. Yes, I am. What do you want, Sabri?'

'Missus Johnston, she is in trouble. She wish to go to Corfu queek.'

He switched the engine off. 'Mrs Johnston is back?' Relief and excitement pulsed through his voice. So she had not gone out in the early hours with Cary and those villainous-looking characters on the cruiser!

'Yes. She come now. Very tired. Very upset. She go to her room.'

'Okay, Sabri. Thanks for telling me.' Paul stepped out of the car, dropped the keys into his pocket and crossed the road. Thank God he knew where he was, now. Thank God and Barrington and the loquacious old Aunt Lucilla Godfrey whom Barrington, with his bloodhound scent, had at last run to ground. He had cursed Barrington for slowness but he had, as usual, done a good job. The telegram had been here when he returned from Lakones at nine o'clock. It had more than made up for the shock of finding the bird had flown from the ramshackle little house with its tell-tale signs of a child's occupation and the suitcase stuffed in the hedge. At least he had been able to tell London that the child was safe. Now that Alix was not Dora, he had said to himself, he could come out into the open and question her.

That was, until he had waited long enough for her appearance at breakfast and gone to her room to investigate. Until he faced the horror of the possibility that she had gone with Cary on the cruiser.

Paul took the steps two at a time. He went along to Alix's door and knocked. The door was ajar and he could hear the shower running. He slipped through his own room and out of the glass doors on to the balcony. He stood at the railing where he could be seen when she emerged from the bathroom. He lit a cigarette. He needed it. He was in the curious situation of being caught up in relief and excitement that, in the circumstances, he had no right to feel, for he had a job to do.

Under the shower Alix was thinking: The message isn't important any longer, now that Cary can't get away. The situation was starting to sort itself out in her mind. What I have to do is find somewhere to take Cary and Benjamin. A secluded house, well away from Paleocastritsa, with a big garden, so that Benjamin would be happy if the south westerly continued. She would hire it for a week. The season had barely begun. There must be plenty of places to let. And she would hire a car. Dora's telephone call would just have to wait. There was no longer any great hurry for that. The important thing was for Benjamin to have somewhere to lay his head tonight.

She dried herself feverishly and went back into the bedroom with the towel round her. 'Paul!' she said the name aloud in shock and nearly dropped her towel. There he was standing on the balcony calmly smoking, like a cat waiting for a mouse. Mesmerized, she went to the door, not knowing what she was going to say, only that she had to face him and it might as well be now. 'Hallo, Paul.'

He looked up and saw her, bare golden shoulders, long bare legs. She looked tired and vulnerable and big-eyed with guilt and surprise. Her hair was wet.

'We-ll hallo.' He crossed the terrace to her door. 'So, you did let me down!'

Alix said nervously: 'No caiques were able to go to sea. When I saw there was a strong south westerly blowing I knew the picnic was off.'

Their eyes met and neither wanted to go on with the charade. Paul said: 'I'm just going off to Corfu. I wondered—'

'Oh! You're offering me a ride! It's exactly

what I need. I was wondering how I was going to get there.'

'Oh?' he looked at her shrewdly. 'Something urgent?'

'I have to put a call through to London.' She would get him to drop her at the post office, then she would give him the slip.

'Okay,' he said. 'Don't hurry. There's plenty of time.'

But there was not plenty of time for what she had to do. And she had not the slightest idea where to find an estate agent. She pulled the curtains across and whisked a thin pair of jeans out of the wardrobe, pulled a sweater over her head, flipped a comb through her hair and outlined her mouth with lipstick. She took her own passport out of the drawer. Heavens alive! She had not repaid Brian Langley the 700 drachmas she had borrowed. She put her travellers cheques and both passports in her shoulder bag, threw the lipstick, comb and a handkerchief, pencil and diary after it, and slid her feet into a pair of light sandals. Ouch! How her feet hurt! She went on to the balcony and said: 'Ready!'

# CHAPTER EIGHTEEN

'You were mighty quick,' observed Paul, smiling. He had thought her beautiful when he suspected she might be Cary Johnston's wife. Now, allowing himself free rein with his emotions for the first time, he found her exquisite.

'I didn't want to hold you up.'

'You needn't have worried. There's plenty of time.' He decided not to ask her where she had been. He did not want to make her lie and they had reached the point of no return now. The lord knew what was going to happen. By the time he found out the cruiser had gone it had been too late to warn Hallow and Jensen whose plane was due to leave Heathrow around mid-day. It was nearly mid-day before, fuming around in the big hotel overlooking the bay, he eventually got through on the telephone. The lines had been very busy, they said. Anyway, even with Cary Johnston half way to wherever he was going, Hallow and Jensen might not turn round and go back to Scotland Yard. What Paul did want to know, and was nervous about asking, was how much Alix knew about Dora.

The drive to Corfu did not provide a fertile bed for conversation. Alix was too concerned with her particular problems. How was she going to give Paul the slip? What she would do if all the house agents were closed? What if Paul clung to her like a leech? She was shaken by the fact that he had not asked her where she had gone this morning. Did that mean he had found the little house and some proof of Cary's recent occupation?

She was emotionally disturbed, too, by her desperate need for someone to confide in, someone to turn to for help. Why don't I talk to him about Cary? The question rose in her mind time and time again, but there was no answer. Whatever Cary had done, he was Tim's cousin. For Tim's sake, she did owe Cary a certain loyalty. At least, now that Cary could not get away, the fear of his taking Benjamin had been shelved. Held up on an island while the wind blew itself out, if the police in England had made some advance in their enquiries, Cary might well be arrested anyway. She was sure she would be clearer in her mind once she had spoken to Dora. But where was she going to contact her? Now that Dora had thrown in the sponge, would she return to Richmond Hill? It was the only address Alix had.

Paul broke the charged silence. 'Have you been to the church of St. Spiridon yet?'

'No.'

'It's worth seeing. It wasn't touched by the

181

shelling of 1944.'

'That's one of the miracles?' She was thinking that she could do with a miracle. Perhaps she ought to go along and put her name on a candle. A wish that Cary would release Benjamin? Or that Dora might suddenly turn up to claim him?

Paul grinned. 'I guess so. He also cures croup, diphtheria and lice. And he is said to have dispersed the attacking Turks at one time, disguised as a south-westerly squall.' He cast her a side-long, careful look and though there was laughter in his voice he was watchful as a lynx. 'Do you suppose today's south westerly is one of his miracles?'

She knew then that he assumed Cary had gone. But she could not talk about it.

He drove up through the new town and parked outside a large, new building.

'Are you leaving the car here?'

'No. This is the OTE, where you telephone. Calls are made from OTEs in Greece.'

'Oh!' The flat exclamation came involuntarily.

'You did say you wanted to telephone.'

'Oh yes. Yes.'

'I'll wait for you.'

'Please, don't do that. It may take ages to get through. I could meet you later.'

He gave her a level look, but his mouth was twitching. 'Could you? Third time

182

lucky, you mean?'

She opened the door and stepped out. She was too strung up to cope with a battle of wits. 'Why don't you leave me to make my own way back?'

'I wouldn't dream of it.'

'Yes, really. I've half a mind to hire a car, anyway.'

He looked suddenly so let down she felt a pang of remorse. 'Won't you let me drive you?'

'It's kind of you, but you have business to attend to. I'd really rather like to be independent.'

Paul was thinking: It's true, I am going to be tied up tomorrow with Hallow and Jensen and the Consul and the Corfu police. 'All right,' he agreed reluctantly. 'When you've made your call I'll take you round to Alexandra Avenue. There is a big car hire firm there.'

'Please. I don't want to bother you any more. You have already been so kind.'

Her hand was on the open window. Paul put his over it. 'More kind than you deserve, you mean? Yes. But I want to know you better.'

She gave him a fleeting little smile and limped up the steps, for the blister was very sore. Well, she could let him take her to Alexandra Avenue. Afterwards, in her own vehicle, she would be free. She could ask the whereabouts of a house agent, drive somewhere near to his office and park safely, unrecognized.

Meantime, she was stuck with this phone call. Perhaps it was for the best. She was not running short of time, yet.

★　　　★　　　★

The phone was ringing. It rang for a long time and Alix's spirits began to sink. Then a woman's voice answered. 'Hallo?'

'Dora!' There was silence and Alix thought she had been cut off. 'Dora? Are you there? Is that you, Dora?'

The voice, sounding shaky and strange, said: 'Who is that, please?' The line, thankfully, was clear.

'My name is Alix Johnston. I am a cousin of the family. I am ringing from Corfu. Could you tell me where I could contact Mrs Johnston, please?'

'Then you don't know, Miss!'

'Don't know what?'

'Mrs Johnston was found.'

'Oh, I'm so glad. May I speak to her?'

'You don't understand, Miss. Her body was found. And now they're looking for the little boy.'

Alix felt herself go rigid. She opened her mouth to speak and no sound came. Then she was gabbling incoherently. 'What

184

happened? What on earth happened? An—an—accident? Benjamin is here. Benjamin is not dead. *Not* dead, do you understand. He was not with his mother. Why don't you know?' Half fainting, her mind was swimming through a grotesque kaleidoscope of pictures. Tim, unidentifiable among the wreckage of his car! A plane crashing as Dora flew to Corfu! Dora, ludicrously in disguise, smashed as she thumbed a lift on the M1. Somewhere among the muddled guessing there was a cold, black, coherent fact trying to get through, but she dared not face it. The voice at the other end had begun to speak again.

'I dare say you are upset, Miss. I'm sorry to tell you like this. I'm the housekeeper. You're Mr Tim's widow, I guess.'

'Yes, Mrs Midgley.' Out of the black confusion, ludicrously, she remembered the woman's name.

'What did you say about the little boy?'

'He's here. He's safe. He's in Corfu.'

'Oh! You've got him. God be praised, dear. I'll tell the police. Will you be bringing him home, then?'

'Yes. Of course. He is with his father. We will all come.' Cary would go back now. Poor Cary! Poor little boy! The tears were escaping down her cheeks and with their release she began to calm a little. 'Tell me what happened to Mrs Johnston. I shall have

185

to tell her husband.' Silence. 'Hallo, Mrs Midgley, can you hear me?'

She scarcely took in the rest. The voice sounded faint, frightened, bewildered. 'I don't know what to say ... There's a warrant out for Mr Johnston's arrest. They say he did it. They say he killed her, before he ran away ...'

\*     \*     \*

The car was empty and it was possible to escape. Alix scarcely remembered crossing the road on some self-protective instinct, skimming past the shops, and diving down an alley. She had seen Paul, a glimpse only as he stood by a kiosk glancing at a newspaper. It was possible he had not seen her. She had to have time to think before facing him.

She ran, bumping into people without apology, regaining her balance and running on. 'They say he killed her, before he ran away ... They say he killed her ... killed her ...' She did not hear the car horns, the angry voices advising her to watch where she was going, the shriek of brakes. Now she was at the main square and there were the colonnades, the rows of chairs and tiny tables; the idle chatterers with their apéritifs. She wondered numbly how life could be going on like this so lightheartedly when such terrible things were happening.

She swung left, hurrying by the colonnades with the restaurants on one side and the great square on the other. There were seats under the trees and seats outside the restaurants. Nowhere to hide when Paul came after her. She needed time to bring herself to her senses and decide what to do.

She turned at the next corner, heading back into the old town along a street enclosed by tall Renaissance buildings. She came out in a tiny square. There before her were grey stone steps leading up to the doorway of an unassuming church.

She went towards them. Though she was not religious, not even a church-goer, she thought instinctively of the church as a refuge. She went unhesitatingly up the steps. An old woman in voluminous black, seated on a stool by the entrance, handed her a printed card. She fumbled in her bag and brought out some drachmas. 'Eengleesh?' Alix nodded. 'Is Spiridon miracles.'

Alix glanced down at the card, saw the lettering and moved it aside. 'I don't know Greek.' The woman pressed the card into her hand and she went on into the darkened interior. Surely this was not the church of St. Spiridon, this hidden place tucked into the middle of the town? She had expected something large and grand. St. Spiridon, giver of miracles. It was going to take a good deal more than a miracle to bring Dora back.

People were coming in behind her. Solemn men and black clad women in the long skirts and head scarves of the town peasants moved down quietly towards a little chapel on the right of the altar. She followed them numbly as far as the grille, then paused. People pushed past her and she stood aside while they went in single file into the sanctuary. There was a mummy, upright in a richly decorated sarcophagus, his small, deep-set eyes peering grotesquely at her out of a wrinkled face. The men and women bent down to kiss the mummy's tiny feet, murmuring their requests, crossing themselves, then returning up the aisle, their faces suffused with simple warmth and happiness.

St. Spiridon had chased the great plague of Naples out of Corfu and expelled epilepsy from the Armenian quarter. Once, as Paul had said, in the guise of a south-westerly squall, he had dispersed the Turkish ships as they came in to attack. His miracle for Benjamin, this driving of the cruiser *Venus* out to sea? A man paused beside her, indicating that she precede him. She went forward uncertainly and touched the rich silver casket. This might be mumbo-jumbo in her sophisticated world, but there were times when she was unwilling to take chances. Anyway, did a small gesture of thanks ever really go amiss?

At the back of the church she paused, turned aside, and sat down on a bench in the gloom to think things out. But she could not think. It was as though the shock of Dora's murder had brought on a retreat from reality and she could only stare blankly at the moving queue of human beings, piously coming and going through the gloomy church between the weird little mummy and the door.

## CHAPTER NINETEEN

Paul found her there. He sat down beside her and gently took her hand in his. 'I saw you running,' he said. 'You run fast for a girl with a blister. They told you? Someone told you on the phone?' He had a folded newspaper in one hand. He tapped it with a forefinger.

She clasped his hand convulsively. The last half hour had shown her she could not face up to this thing alone. She had never been so glad to see anyone in her life.

He drew her hand into the curve of his arm, holding it close against him. 'Come with me,' he said.

His gentleness broke through the black void that hid her mind and memory. A tear

189

escaped and ran down her cheek. 'I've been looking after him,' she said. Her voice trembled.

'I know. We must talk.'

'Paul, I can hardly walk.' She was crying. It was easier to think about her feet than the other thing. The blister had broken while she ran. It was clinging wetly, painfully, to the inside of her sandal.

He dried her tears with a large handkerchief. 'Let's find a chemist.' She went with him, limping, her mind obsessively on the blister. They purchased some Elastoplast and next door at a little shoe shop he bought her a pair of rope sandals. 'Not very elegant,' he said, 'but good for the hills.'

The tears spilled over again. The proprietor of the shop, a middle-aged man with dark Greek hair, grey English eyes and a sensitive face, put a hand on her shoulder and asked concernedly: 'The lady has trouble?'

'She has had some bad news.'

'Ah! I am sorry. One moment.' He went out into the street and came back with a small glass of golden liquid. 'Brandy. It will do you good.'

She gulped it down and felt better. 'I'm sorry.' She dashed a hand across her eyes. 'I've been in pieces.'

'I'm not surprised. Come, I'll take you to a

bar and we'll have another.'

The man nodded sympathetically. 'Brandy is good.'

'Yes.'

Carrying her sandals, Paul led her back to the square and chose a table under the trees. There was no one sitting near. A waiter came and he ordered two coffees with brandy. 'You will feel better after this. Would you like to eat something?'

She shook her head. 'I couldn't, thank you all the same.'

She fingered the edge of her glass. 'Did you follow me out here? I mean, did you know I was on that plane?' She looked up into those very alert blue eyes within their dark lashes, at the very masculine face softened now by compassion for her. His dark hair had fallen across his forehead as it always did when the wind touched it. After the treacherous, haunted look of Cary, he appeared infinitely honest and kind.

'No. I work for an insurance company. I came to look for Johnston.'

'I knew. I saw it in that paper Nico brought you last night.'

He gave her a wry smile. 'I guessed that was the reason for your early morning flit. My company sent me out here to investigate the possibility that, against all the odds, Cary Johnston was holed-up in Corfu. Everyone said he'd never come here. That he'd go to

South America, or Australia. But one of the directors had a bee in his bonnet about Corfu. He said Johnston was a greedy man and greedy men chance their luck. He knew about the arms traffic. You know about that?'

She nodded. 'I do now.'

'This chap put forward the theory that a complicated matter involving money coming from the Middle East to, say, a Swiss bank, with contacts in various countries running various boats, a train of events would be set up that might be impossible to hurry and difficult to cancel. He was pinning his hopes on the possibility that there was a deal in progress at the time Cary disappeared. And he would be tempted to risk completing it.'

'Guesswork?'

'Not entirely. A bit of sleuthing was involved. He had obtained the dates of Cary's various trips to Corfu and they fell into a pattern. So I was sent out to have a nose around. I was standing in the luggage queue at the Olympic desk at Heathrow, looking round in a bored sort of way when I spotted you. You seemed to be making for the same queue and I thought: Ha! Pretty girl going to Corfu, too!'

'Really? Is that all?'

It had been all at the time, but that was a century of emotion ago. Even by the time they were half way to Corfu he had been aware that she was shifting subtly in his mind. Out of the category of a good lay into some area of his mind that he could not tabulate and scarcely understood. 'Then you shot off to the coffee room and as I hate standing in queues I thought I'd push off and ogle you for ten minutes.'

'Oh Paul!' She laughed softly and the laughter brought a tear or two of sheer weakness. She fingered them away. 'Aunt Lucilla had a bad foot. I didn't want her to stand around. But the fact that you did single me out at Heathrow—Isn't it too much of a coincidence?'

'There's a coincidence in the fact that I should get the same flight as my quarry's cousin, but that's what we in the business call luck. You're no good in this sort of job if you don't attract at least your fair share of luck. I do. But I was baffled when I found who you were, until a friend in the police ran your aunt, Mrs Godfrey, to ground. She swears you didn't know Cary was here.'

'I didn't.' She told him about coming upon Benjamin on the beach. 'He had had enough of being imprisoned up at Lakones and he ran away.' Paul had put the newspaper on the table. She drew it towards her ... The headline was in heavy black print.

*Financier's wife found?* Her flesh crawled as she read on. *The search for Cary Johnston, the financier who disappeared a fortnight ago, was stepped up today after the body of a woman was found by workmen in a disused culvert a quarter of a mile from the Johnston home on Richmond Hill this evening. Police investigating refuse to either confirm or deny that the body was that of Mrs Dora Johnston, who went missing at the same time as her husband.*

'But it is her,' Alix whispered, 'I talked to their housekeeper.'

He nodded. 'I telephoned this morning after finding the hide-out empty.'

'We went to Castel Angelo.'

Paul started violently. 'You mean, *he didn't get away on the* Venus?'

'He didn't know *Venus* was in until I told him.'

Paul whistled. 'I didn't realize...'

'I had made an arrangement with them to bring Cary down at nine o'clock tonight. Then the south westerly blew up in the early hours and the cruiser had to leave.'

'Well! There's a turn-up for the books,' Paul remarked with satisfaction.

'Paul, he's got Benjamin.' She pushed her chair back. 'I've got to go. I've got to do something. I can't leave him with the child now I know—'

He reached for her hand and pulled her back. 'Sit down. We've got to talk this right through. So Johnston is here! Now tell me, why Castel Angelo?'

194

'I don't know. It was a hiding place. I told Cary about you and he took fright.'

'Castel Angelo! A hiding place!' Paul echoed in disbelief. 'People go up there.'

'Not many. It's such a climb.'

'They go, all the same,' Paul replied in a puzzled voice.

'Tourists?'

'Yes. Very energetic holidaymakers climb up there for the view. Not many, I'll grant you, but the point I am making is Cary couldn't count on *nobody* coming. I can't understand why he would want to go there. His face is so familiar to the English public now. It's been all over every paper in the past few weeks. Anyone might recognize him—especially since the child is with him.'

'He could see the track,' she offered uncertainly. 'He would have warning. And Paul, he has a gun.'

'But who wants to sit on the top of a peak watching a track all day? Even holding a gun. Especially with a little boy to entertain. If he wanted to hide, there are plenty of places in the hills.'

The waiter came with the drinks. Espresso coffee and two glasses of brandy. They sat in silence until he had gone away.

Paul frowned at his glass. 'I can't understand it. There's got to be a clue. Who were those chaps on the cruiser? How did you come to know them?'

She told him about meeting Scunthorpe at the party at Richmond Hill

'Where are they taking him? Do you know?'

'Africa.' She gave a little moan. 'The terrible thing is, in my heart I knew he had done something ghastly. He had to have, to be afraid of extradition. And I knew all the time there was something strange about Dora. She was so fond of Benjamin.'

'Wasn't Cary?'

'Yes, I thought so. But obviously it didn't suit him to have the child all to himself. He's impatient with him. I kept thinking Dora wouldn't send Benjamin off like that with Cary, with scarcely any clothes and no toys. It was all very strange, but I was in such a stew about Benjamin I couldn't put my mind to what was behind it all.'

'Africa!' said Paul thoughtfully. 'He seems to have a stake in dissidents. He has a nose for locating the illegal element.'

'Anarchists?'

Paul nodded. 'The people who, by the very nature of their undertakings, have to pay a high price for firearms.'

'I can't believe Dora knew about this,' said Alix in distress.

'Drink your brandy,' he advised gently. 'Was she the sort of person who was prepared to go where the money was good and not ask questions?'

'Perhaps. I'm not sure. She was silly, in a way.'

'From what I've heard, she liked to throw money around.'

'Wouldn't we all, if we had it?' Alix asked wryly.

Paul said softly: 'You're extraordinarily loyal. It's one of the things I like about you.' He took her hand again. 'There are so many things I like about you.'

Tears filled her eyes again and she gripped his hand convulsively. 'I am so glad to have you. Paul, why do they think Cary killed her?'

'There was evidence, it seems. There is no doubt in the minds of the police. They put out a warrant immediately for his arrest. The Fraud Squad was about to issue a warrant anyway, for the money affair.'

'Can the Corfu police arrest him?'

'It depends on what arrangements are made. They can certainly detain him for questioning. He came in on a false passport.' Paul looked enquiringly at Alix. 'Fuller?'

'You knew? Yes, of course you knew. You looked in my handbag last night at the Circe.'

'Forgive me.'

'I have it here.' She drew the passport out of her bag. 'He wants me to go to the post office for some message. It's terribly important to him. He doesn't want to go

197

without it.'

Paul opened the folder and examined the pages. 'Benjamin is on this.'

'I don't understand it,' Alix said. 'Cary could so easily have dumped Benjamin on a relation, telling them he and Dora were going abroad.'

'Is it that easy? The boy is old enough to say his mother disappeared. That she didn't say goodbye. A man would make mistakes in the packing of his clothes. And there's one very nasty little possibility that occurs to me. A man who kills his wife is capable of using his son as a hostage.'

Alix clapped a hand to her mouth. 'Oh! My God!'

'One has to think of these things,' Paul said gently. 'Why is he here on Corfu when he could have flown straight to North Africa? If the hunch my boss had is right, and he is here to tie up an arms deal, he knew before leaving home there was a possibility of time running out for him. Rumours from Corfu seeping back to England. Dora's body being found. And such outside disasters as the weather letting him down, as it has. It has come to a point where he is walking on a razor's edge and he may have foreseen that. He may have deliberately planned to use the boy if he had to. And there's something significant, surely, in his being on top of that hill with a gun.'

She put her hands over her face.

'But after all,' Paul put in gently, 'Benjamin is his own son.'

She took her hands away and looked at him with raw fear. 'Dora was his own wife.'

'It may be easier to kill a wife than one's flesh and blood. Besides, we don't know how Dora died. It may have been unpremeditated. Johnston was bound to have been in a highly emotional state, when he was on the brink of arrest. Let's count him semi-innocent until proved guilty, shall we?'

He picked up the passport and flicked it between his fingers. 'Sit here and sip that brandy while I go off to the post office to get that very important message. It could be said we're not breaking any rules, now, by opening it.'

## CHAPTER TWENTY

The telegram had been sent from Geneva.
FUNDS FROM J A IN ACCOUNT STOP GOODS READY TUNIS STOP SIGNAL 161 KNEF

Paul anchored it to the table with his glass. 'Does the name Knef mean anything to you?'

'Nothing. It's a German name, isn't it?'

'Possibly Cary's Swiss contact. There will be a syndicate. I'd guess that J A means

Jordanian Arabs. And—161—I suppose they've got a selection of signals with various meanings to cover various eventualities.' Paul frowned. 'The A might mean Anarchists. It comes to the same thing. Anyway, it means, presumably, that the money has been paid and the *Venus* can pick Johnston up and run him over to Tunis, flash signal 161 whatever that may be, and either go in to collect the guns or have them brought out to him.' The smoke from his cigarette quivered away on a breeze. Alix watched it and something turned over in her mind. Paul said, frowning down at the telegram, flicking the edge between finger and thumb: 'Signal ... signal ... I have an idea. This may be the explanation for Cary's making you take him to Castel Angelo. It's an excellent spot to signal from.'

'But he did not need to signal. I was to take him down to the bay at nine o'clock. Paul, I am out of my mind about Benjamin.'

'I know, darling. But there is something I haven't told you. Two men from Scotland Yard are due to land here at six-fifty. I was going in to meet them.'

'And what do you suppose they can do, even if they have made arrangements with the Corfu police? You mentioned taking Cary in for questioning. Cary is on a small pinnacle with a gun...' Paul was exhaling another cloud of smoke. She watched it, her eyes dilating as the wind whisked it away. Now she was certain. She stifled a cry of alarm.

'Paul, the wind has changed. It's blowing from the north.'

Paul swung round in his chair and looked at the trees. 'Yes, it is. So—*Venus* will come in and Johnston will expect you up at the track as arranged. The police will be able to take your place. Stop worrying. I know you've had a hell of a day, but it's going to be all right now.' He looked at his watch. 'It's nearly half past five. Let's go back to the car and drive slowly out to the airport.'

She did not want to go to the airport and get mixed up with the police. She wanted to go back to Paleocastritsa—just in case. Paul took her arm. 'You're shaking.'

'I am nervous. I'm frightened. Paul, I want to go back to Sabri's.'

'No, Alix. You mustn't.' He was afraid she would do something silly. 'I won't let you.'

'What if *Venus* comes in and Cary sees her and comes down and takes Benjamin off with him?'

'He wouldn't. He knows everything is fixed for nine o'clock. Besides, he wants his telegram.' They were walking in through the arch and starting down the busy little shopping street.

'He doesn't trust me. He might panic and run.' She was thinking of Paul's theory about

Castel Angelo. That it was a good place to send signals from. And the fact that part of the yacht basin was visible from the peak.

'Cary Johnston may seem to you to have human aspects, but take it from me, he's got to have nerves of steel for the life he lives.'

'I hope you're right.'

'And I love you.' He held her arm more tightly against his side. 'It's not the moment to say so, I know, but I'm boiling over with it.' He had gone through hell waiting to find out if Alix was Dora. And later, if she was in cahoots with Johnston. He wanted to get this ghastly business cleared up and start wooing her.

Her voice broke tremulously through his dream: 'Don't say such things. There is so much at stake.'

'Nothing so important.' He lifted her hand to his lips. 'Stop worrying about that child. We'll get him out of this all right.'

She wished she had his confidence. He did not know Cary as she knew him.

Paul jingled some coins in his pocket, reminding her of the debt she owed.

'I've forgotten to repay Brian Langley the seven hundred drachmas I borrowed from him. If we pass an open bank or a Bureau de Change, I must cash a traveller's cheque.'

The opportunity offered itself before they came to the square where the car was parked. 'You go on,' she said to Paul and slipped through the door. Taking her cheques and passport from her bag, she went up to the counter. As she handed the papers across she glanced up and saw the Frenchman from Sabri's tucking his wallet into his pocket. He smiled at her. 'Good evening, Madame.'

'Good evening.' And then, on an impulse: 'Are you going back to Paleocastritsa, now?'

'Do you want a lift?'

'I would be very grateful.'

'I'll wait for you. The car is close by.'

'In this square?'

'No. Behind the building. We can go out of the side door...'

★   ★   ★

She should not have done it. She was craven with guilt and unbearably distressed at letting Paul down again, but if she went to the car to tell him, he would not allow her to go. She knew he would not wait long. Within a few moments he would become impatient, or suspicious, hurry over to the Bureau de Change, realize she had given him the slip and be forced to go to the airport alone.

As he had said, it was the third time she had eluded him. He would be angry, and perhaps upset, but not overly surprised. Paul had become very important to her in the few days she had known him, but he was not as important tonight as little Benjamin. If she did not get that poor child away from Cary tonight the picture of his wan, sad face, his thin, lonely figure in the creased jeans, his tousled, unkempt hair, was going to haunt her for the rest of her days.

The Frenchman was a fast driver. Madame made the conversation. Alix answered her probing questions absently, her mind elsewhere. By the time they reached Sabri's she felt ill with apprehension. She murmured her thanks and slipped out of the car. Sabri was waiting around the front of the hotel with his welcoming smile. 'Ah! Missus Johnston! You back soon! What happen Mister Crispin?'

'I—er—I had to leave him.'

'Is trouble again?'

'Well, yes.'

'I have letter for you.'

'A letter?' She followed Sabri to the tiny office. He produced a piece of folded paper along with her room key. Time seemed to stand still. *Gone. Left B. alone C.A. Thanks.* Sheer disbelief! That a man, any man, would leave any small boy, much less his son, alone on top of a cliff! Remember Dora! Her blood chilled. 'Who brought this?'

'Jani Kalocheiritis.'

'Who is he?'

'He have olive trees near Castel Angelo.' She could tell he had read the note but did not understand it. 'The Englishman give him note. Is he friend of you, Missus Johnston?' Sabri was suddenly furtive.

'In a way,' she said. She swung round looking out to sea. The water in the bay had calmed considerably. She asked: 'Is it possible to climb down from Castel Angelo to the water?'

Sabri shook his head, 'Is very steep. Very dangerous.'

Cary diced with danger every day. 'Could a boat come in there? A cruiser?'

He nodded, looking puzzled. 'Water very deep. Better go by road, Missus Johnston. Not safe to climb.'

She remembered Cary's holding up a hand and looking worried when she spoke of the wind. And then he had tried to push her off in a hurry, without lunch. Was there an alternative plan? A safe harbour on the Albanian side of the island, perhaps? He could have hitched a ride, or caught a bus from Lakones to the turn-off, then another bus to somewhere where he could get a taxi. Benjamin could have been alone virtually since she left!

'Give this to Mr Crispin. Tell him I have gone for Benjamin.' She did a quick reconnoitre of the tables by the vine outside the restaurant. There was no sign of the Langleys. No taxis. No bus. She did not feel she could ask a favour of the French couple, and there was no one else she knew. She cast around in mounting despair. The sun was a bloody half-circle on the flat blue line of the horizon. In ten minutes it would be gone and Benjamin would be alone on a mountain top in the creeping dusk that would deepen too quickly tonight. She had to get to Castel Angelo, and she had to get there quickly. She could not think of the relief of Cary's departure, only the terror of a little boy, miles from anywhere. Would Cary shut him in the chapel? Or would he leave him free to stumble around the cliff-top, desperately seeking a way of escape? Then suddenly Alix saw, beneath the big eucalyptus tree, the man who hired out the Lambrettas. She ran diagonally across the road to him.

## CHAPTER TWENTY-ONE

There was, she saw with relief, a pillion seat.

'You want tomorrow?' The man was delighted at the thought of a booking.

'No. I want it now.' He looked doubtful. 'There is a light,' Alix pointed out. 'I am only going to—er—Lakones. I shall have the bike back in an hour or so.'

'You can ride?' He was still reluctant to let it go at this late hour.

'Yes, of course. Please, I am in a hurry.'

He showed her how to start and stop it, and how to work the gears. It was not going to be easy, she could see. She had a fair sense of balance. She slung her bag over her back and it slipped down across her arm. She looked up to see Sabri coming across the road. She tossed it to him. 'Please look after this for me, Sabri.' The engines fired, issued a lightweight snarl, and Alix balanced herself on the seat. 'Okay. I'll be all right, now.' The owner let the machine go and she sped noisily up the road.

It was already dark within the confines of the trees that lined the winding road to Lakones. The little machine was fast and willing, and after all not too difficult to ride. She sped up to the top of the hill, through the village, and out on to the road that led to Castel Angelo. Again, the olive groves nudging up to the road brought their own darkness. She had paused twice, fretting and fuming, before she recognized the spot where the track came in. Ah! There it was! She pulled the machine off the road, ran it down a slope and left it leaning against the contorted trunk of an ancient olive tree.

Why on earth had she not asked Sabri for the loan of a flashlight? She thrust a way between the overgrown bracken that led in beneath the shading olives. Her eyes were growing accustomed to the darkness. She emerged from the olive grove on to the rough

207

track. The moon was out now, a big, not-quite-circular ball and its gold was deepening as the last of the twilight ebbed away. In the bushes she could hear the shuffle of birds and once a nightjar made her jump as it slid by on silent wings.

Was she on the right track? Though the mountain top brooded blackly above, it would take a good deal longer to reach if she came to the base at the wrong angle. There were no landmarks, but, as the moon brightened and a faint powdering of stars appeared in the sky she came, thankfully, upon a little stream that ran along the track for a few yards and where the stones were slippery with moss. She remembered sliding there in the morning and knew with infinite relief that she was on the route. There were tree frogs here, croaking harshly in a small dark tree whose shiny leaves caught a splash of the moon's rays, and another owl drifted across her path as silently as a snowflake.

She was walking painfully now, trying to keep her weight off the blister. She seemed to have been going all her life when she came upon the lower, outer wall of the ruin and paused for breath. Then, in spite of the pain and exhaustion, she put on a spurt, half-running upwards on the narrow track between the stone slabs and massive foundations.

She came over the final rise and there was

the summit, bathed in a pale moon. She stood looking round in the eerie, silvery light and suddenly there was a yelp of delight and Benjamin came dashing across the grass to her. 'Here she is!' he shouted. 'Here she is!' There was a crazy moment of suspended belief, then Cary stepped out from behind a wall.

'Hallo,' he said. 'You're early. Weren't we going to meet you down at the road?'

The agonizing strain, the pent-up terror, the pushing, thrusting fear had taken her last ounce of vitality. She said shakily: 'I got your note.'

'What note?' She stared at him. 'Did you get any mail?' Cary asked.

'Yes. A telegram.' What was he doing here? She must be going out of her mind.

'Poor Alix is tired,' said Benjamin. 'She can ride Aph'dite. Can we go now? I'm tired of this picnic and it's awfully dark.' His waif-look, the look of an unloved child that had struck Alix with such intensity when she first saw him, had come back again.

'We're going soon, darling,' she said.

'Where is the telegram?' asked Cary brusquely.

'I haven't got it.'

'*What?*'

'Cary! Did you send a message down to the hotel for me?'

'No, of course I didn't. What do you mean

you haven't got the telegram? What have you done with it?' She could see the anger, and a leaden fear coming up behind his eyes, and all she could think of was that he had killed Dora. Instinctively, she put an arm round Dora's child.

'*What have you done with my telegram?*'

'Listen, Cary.' Her voice was trembling. 'I received a note. A man called Jani brought it to Sabri's. It said "Gone. Left B. alone C. A. Thanks".'

They faced each other in a loaded silence. Then she said to the child: 'Where are the donkeys?'

He pointed into the darkness beyond the chapel.

'Did you give them some grass?'

'Yes.'

'Run along and see if they have finished it.'

Benjamin moved off reluctantly. 'Can we go home then?'

'Soon.'

Benjamin stopped only a yard away. His pale face was dirty, and Alix saw now that he had been crying for there were tear stains where the dirt had been partially washed away. His blond hair that had grown too long fell in bars across his eyes. He looked up at Alix, then at his father and his face crumpled. 'I wish Mommy would come. I don't like it here.' Alix felt Cary's eyes riveted on her face. She turned her own eyes away because he would read in them what she knew. He must have thought of the possibility of her seeing a newspaper. Even the possibility of Lucilla sending her the news if Dora's body was found. Benjamin started to walk towards the donkeys.

'*Sweet Lass of Richmond Hill*...'

'Shut *up*!' said Cary violently. 'I told you I am sick to death of that song.'

The little boy turned round. The tears were running down his cheeks. 'It's Mommy's song,' he said mutinously. And then he gave a great bellow of childish grief. 'I want my Mom-m-my.'

Alix ran to him, knelt down with her arms round him. 'I am going to take you home tomorrow,' she said. 'We're going to my hotel tonight. Then tomorrow we'll get an aeroplane home.' She dried his tears with a tissue. 'Be a darling and go and see if our donkeys are all right, then we'll go.'

He trotted off obediently, half-sobbing, and she stood up. Cary was close behind her, looking down into her face with narrowed, questioning eyes and she felt her heart thundering. Had he noted the omission of the word Mommy in her promise to rehabilitate Benjamin? He knew she did not lie willingly. Panic-stricken, she flared at him: 'You're lying about that note. You didn't trust me to come back, and so you sent me the note to ensure I would.'

211

His eyes glittered coldly in the moonlight. 'So? You came back.'

She was talking feverishly, angrily. 'But you made a tactical error. You didn't reckon with the fact that I would be so alarmed about Benjamin that I would leave my handbag at the hotel.'

The cold glitter went out of his eyes. His face softened. She had never seen anything so deliberate, or for that matter, so phony in her life. 'Don't worry, my dear. You can go and get it later when we keep the appointment at the cruiser.'

It was a situation she might have dreamed up. She took the greatest pleasure in saying: 'You've put yourself into my hands now, with your unfair suspicions. I can leave Benjamin at the hotel when I get the telegram. You see, I don't trust you, either.'

'But, my dear Alix,' Cary replied suavely, 'I told you I would leave him with you. Why should you doubt my word?'

She did not want to talk to him. She wanted to think about what was going to happen if Paul returned to Sabri's, found Cary's note, and came dashing up here to help her. But there was no reason for Cary to pull his gun on Paul. If everyone kept his head, it was a situation that could work. She turned her back on Cary and went over to the donkeys to be with Benjamin. A new thought struck her. Paul knew the time of

212

the rendezvous at the yacht basin. He was bound to bring the police. They would look at the message and then check to see if *Venus* had come and gone. Since Cary was prepared to go on with last night's plan, presumably *Venus* was there. She shivered.

Cary's footsteps were crunching on the stony ground behind her. She swung round nervously. 'It's time to go,' he said. He went into the little chapel and came out carrying the pannier bag that must contain his possessions and the gun. He slung it over Heracles's back, then hesitated. 'We might as well leave the donkeys here.'

Angry at his callousness in abandoning them, Alix did not stop to think. 'You're going to need them,' she said. 'I didn't bring the car.' She could have bitten her tongue out then. The time for Cary to find there was no car was when they reached the road, for Paul might be there, and the police.

'Didn't bring the car!' Cary swung round, his face livid in the cold moonlight.

She kept her voice as steady as she was able. 'I told you you messed things up by sending that stupid note. I hired a scooter.'

He came towards her. 'You left the car there and hired a scooter!' he exclaimed, furious, incredulous.

'I—I didn't hire a car.'

'Why?' The word came like a pistol shot.

'B-because I—I got a ride out from Corfu.

213

Then your note was there and I looked round for someone to bring me, and there was no one, so I hired a scooter.'

Dear God, she had made a mess of things! There had been time to think out a plausible story, but she had not done it because she was so emotionally involved with the child.

Cary grasped her arms, his fingers biting into the flesh. She wanted to cry out but she was afraid of frightening Benjamin. Her face twisted with pain. 'You weren't coming to get me, were you?' His thumbs pressed agonizingly, torturing her into lightheadedness. 'Come out with it, little cousin,' Cary said with deadly emphasis. 'What happened when you went into Corfu today?'

## CHAPTER TWENTY-TWO

As Paul ran the car down the hill he saw *Venus* coming into the little bay. 'It's evidently been standing off all day,' he said.

The Greek inspector sat forward on his seat peering out of the window. 'Mr Crispin, I think I leave you at the next bend. I walk over to the Circe. I know the owner.'

'Okay. I'll drop you.'

The man turned to look out of the rear window. 'We seem to have left the other cars

214

behind. You're a fast driver.'

'When necessary.' He whirled round the remaining bends and stopped a hundred yards short of Sabri's. 'What about you two?' He turned to John Hallow. 'Do you want to go over to the Circe?'

'I'd like to have a word with Mrs Johnston. What time did you say she has this appointment?'

'Eight.'

He glanced at his watch. 'I'll slip along and see her now. If she hasn't already gone.'

Benson said: 'I'll wait here for our friends.' He and the Greek officer climbed out, the Greek adjusting his holster on his hip. Paul put the car into gear and ran on down to the hotel.

'Nice place,' said Hallow, looking interestedly through the open window. All the coloured lights were on, glowing from their beds of vine, and the candles in their flower posies on the white-clothed tables sent up dozens of tiny flames. The guests, gay in long, bright dresses and casual shirts, lounged over apéritifs on the narrow forecourt. Brian Langley looked up and waved. Paul jumped out and went over to him. 'Have you seen Alix?'

'Not a sign. Someone said they saw her disappear with you.'

'She came back.' He strode towards the office and there was Sabri emerging from

215

beneath the tall palm by the bougainvillaea, picturesque as his surroundings in black with his white frilled shirt, black tie and red cummerbund. Sabri eyed him suspiciously.

'Sabri! Has Mrs Johnston been in?'

It seemed he had made a mistake this afternoon in dropping the lovely Mrs Johnston into this man's lap.

'Missus Johnston leave note for you.' He went into the office and produced it, watching Paul's face warily as he unfolded the piece of paper and his astonished eyes took in the words. *Gone. Left B. alone C. A. Thanks.*

Paul put a hand across his eyes as though he could block out the sight of his whole world disintegrating before him. He could not believe it and yet, yes he could—well almost. She had eluded him once too often and it had crossed his mind there in the Bureau de Change that perhaps, after all, the sort of love a loyal girl like Alix could give a man might surmount even murder.

That she was shocked by Dora's death there was no doubt in his mind. She had not been playing a part in Corfu. And yet, she had been willing to go off with the murderer! Paul stared down at the message and thought bitterly: I don't know much about women, after all. She made all that fuss about the boy, and yet, when it came to running away with his father, she actually left

216

him alone in an appallingly dangerous spot with darkness coming on!

He looked up into Sabri's closed face, his curious dark eyes. Something seemed to burst inside him and he said angrily: 'Is this all?' He thrust the piece of paper under Sabri's nose. 'Is this really all?'

'She say she gone to get—' Sabri hesitated. He could not remember that unfamiliar name, and he was not certain he would be able to pronounce it if he did.

Paul stared at him, waiting. Sabri did not like his aggressiveness, his anger. Even if he could remember the name, he decided suddenly, he would not tell Crispin. The man had a car, Mrs Johnston, a slow Lambretta.

'Okay,' snapped Paul. 'I know.' The Greek devil! Perhaps he had acted as go-between all the time. He remembered the dancing when Sabri had led Alix off. He had said she was the prettiest girl in the room. Well, she had been, but it was good cover-up stuff, all the same. Sabri must be Johnston's ally. Of course, that made sense of Alix's coming here. No wonder Sabri had been so bloody unfriendly and hadn't wanted him to stay in the first place. He might have spotted that if—it was true, what Barrington always said. Don't get involved with a girl on a job.

He looked up and saw Hallow strolling across the road towards him. He said tersely:

217

'There is a note here for me saying Alix and Johnston have done a flit together and left the boy at Castel Angelo.'

'*What!*'

Paul snapped: 'I was wrong. Have you ever been fooled by a woman?'

Hallow stared at him in consternation. 'But—the cruiser is only just coming in.'

'Maybe they decided, when Alix turned up with the news that you were on your way, to take a different route. It makes sense. She must have grabbed a car, made a dash for the mountain and whipped him off.' Paul added angrily: 'The child was too much of a burden, it seems. I had better get up there fast and bring him down before some disaster hits the poor little devil.' He swore violently under his breath. It did nothing to ease the pain. 'And by the way, Sabri, my host—' he turned at the same moment as Sabri turned and they eyed each other malevolently '—would appear to be in on this. You might tip off the Greeks. They ought to question him.'

'Right! But what about the Johnstons!' Hallow swung round, pointing over the isthmus towards the yacht anchorage. 'Why shouldn't they be in that olive grove now, waiting to jump aboard?'

'Yes, they'll be there—if they've taken leave of their senses,' Paul retorted sarcastically. 'There's nothing stupid about

Alix, let me tell you, and you know what sort of brain Johnston's got. Maybe the *Venus* is a decoy. Maybe they've got another boat taking them off. Or, on the other hand, they may have taken to the hills. I don't see them going into Corfu. The town's too small.' He crumpled the note in his hand and pushed it down into his pocket. 'Anyway, that's your pigeon, Hallow. I'm off to collect this poor little kid.' It would give him something to get his teeth into. He had no heart for helping the police now. He had given them all the information he had. And he did not want to be around when they brought Alix in. God in heaven! She had taken on something in her blind passion for that scoundrel. He wondered how long this situation had been going on, and if it was behind Dora's murder. No wonder she had been so upset in Corfu! No wonder she had run away. She had to gather her wits and ask herself if she could really go along with murder! It hadn't taken her long to make up her mind. Was that what she had been doing in the church? Asking God's guidance! Sakes alive.

Brian Langley said: 'I think there's something wrong over there. I'm going to see if there is anything I can do.'

Jane said wryly: 'Are you thinking your seven hundred drachmas might have gone off?'

The doctor rose from his chair. 'I am

keeping an open mind about that. I think I had better find out if Paul has seen today's paper.'

There was a shriek of brakes, a Greek expletive, and Paul regained his balance, missing the front bumper of a cruising taxi by a hair's breadth. He had been saying to himself that he wasn't going to cry over a woman he was well rid of, but in fact he must have been pretty near to it or he would have seen that bloody car.

'Lunatic!'

'Go to hell,' he snarled. He opened his car door and slid behind the wheel. As he turned on the ignition, a hand touched his shoulder. He was suddenly aware of a burst of startled chatter from the terrace. Everyone had seen and heard the incident with the taxi. The hell with them, too, if they were that short of entertainment, he thought savagely.

'Paul! Is something the matter?'

He could not answer. He stared grimly straight ahead. Dr Langley was accustomed to seeing people in varying states of shock. He said: 'You don't look as though you ought to be driving, old chap. Can I help?'

Paul said in a carefully controlled voice, still looking out in front: 'Dora Johnston was murdered and Alix has run off with Cary. They left the little boy on Castel Angelo. I am going to get him.'

Nothing human beings did surprised Brian

Langley. Ten years as a GP in a country village had taught him more than he needed to know about what they could do to each other. 'Have you got a flashlight?' he asked.

'No.'

'I'll see if I can borrow one from Sabri and come with you.'

## CHAPTER TWENTY-THREE

'Let Alix go!' Benjamin began pummelling at Cary's legs. 'You're hurting her.'

Alix could scarcely get her breath for the pain but she managed to gasp: 'I'll tell you. I'll tell you, if you let me go.'

'Why did you do that?' shouted Benjamin, his little face flushed with indignation.

'Because she has been a naughty girl,' replied Cary softly, malevolently, his eyes never leaving Alix's white face.

'No, she hasn't been naughty. She has not!' asserted Benjamin. 'Please, Daddy, can't we go back to the house?'

Alix picked him up in her arms. It gave her an opportunity to turn away from Cary and gather her wits. She said: 'We're going to my hotel tonight, and tomorrow I'll take you home on an aeroplane.'

He gave a yelp of delight. 'Home to Mommy!'

She tried to say yes but the word stuck against an enormous lump that threatened to choke her. She tried to get it over the lump and eventually it came, mangled and queer, a total give-away.

'So that's it!' Cary's words were an accusation. 'You know!'

She swung round to him, her face twisted with fear. 'Why don't you go? Go anywhere. Do what you want to do, only leave me to take Benjamin down to Sabri's. I won't tell anyone. I won't talk to anyone. I promise.'

'You won't have to, will you, cousin Alix. They know, don't they?'

'I don't know what you mean.' She tried not to look at him but she was drawn by his hostility. He looked brutal, with his face cold and framed by the black stubble of beard.

'They've found Dora, haven't they? Well, haven't they?'

The donkeys, hobbled close by, moved restlessly.

'Yes. I saw it in the paper.'

'No, little cousin. You say "I saw it in the paper" too fast. You must learn to lie with more panache.'

'Please, take me home.' Benjamin had begun to whimper. 'I'm tired of this picnic.'

Alix pressed his head against her shoulder. 'We'll go soon.'

'Put him down,' Cary ordered her. 'I want to talk to you.'

Benjamin's head flopped from sheer exhaustion.

'In a moment, when I am sure he is asleep. Would you arrange the pannier bags on the chapel floor? Double them one on the other, and I'll lay him there.'

Cary took her by the arm, propelling her forward, then he picked up the bags and spread them impatiently. 'Okay. Put him down.'

She did so, and he did not stir. Cary jerked his head towards the door.

Now that the first shock was over, she was thinking again. She was willing to co-operate to the fullest degree to ensure she and Benjamin came out of this alive. They were standing on the cliff-top facing over Paleocastritsa. The lights of the Scheria twinkled on the edge of the bay and across the isthmus two single golden pin-points indicated the position of the Circe and the little dwelling close by. Here and there on the silent hill, villa and hotel lights had sprung up. The two big hotels glittered like monstrous, misshapen Christmas trees. 'Let's have it,' said Cary.

'I rang your home,' Alix began. 'Mrs Midgeley told me Dora's body had been found.'

He only said: 'Go on.'

'She said there was a warrant out for your arrest. Then I saw it in the paper.' She could no longer look at him. She thought of Tim, and the way Cary had looked like Tim when she saw him at the hideout. She remembered with disgust how she had not protested too much that time he kissed her.

'What else?' Cary rapped the words out impatiently.

'If I tell you all I know, will you go away and leave me here with Benjamin?'

'I make the conditions,' he replied. 'Get on with the story.'

'Tell me it was an accident.' In a way, it did not really matter if he lied. Dora's murder was so unacceptable, she needed, illogically, reasons, excuses.

'It was an accident.' He said the words mechanically. 'What the hell, Alix! She's dead. It doesn't matter how it happened. Stop looking at me like that. It's the living that count. Can't you understand, it's *too late* for Dora!'

And it was. Cary was right. She had only to face up to the fact.

She said: 'I got a ride into Corfu with Paul—'

'The insurance chap?'

'Yes.'

'He was going to the airport to meet some police. I got a lift back with some other people from the hotel. When I arrived Sabri gave me the note. That's all there is to tell.' Wild horses would not have dragged out of her the wording of the telegram.

Cary was looking at her keenly. 'If you hadn't found the note you wouldn't have come.'

She lifted her eyes to his. 'I don't know what I would have done. Cary, believe me when I say I am not interested in you. I only want you to give me Benjamin.'

He might not have heard her for all the reaction he gave. 'So they know I am up here?'

'Paul will have told them.'

'And what time was the plane due?'

She was afraid to lie to him. In the moonlight his eyes were a little mad. Anyway, he probably knew. They arrived at the same time every day. 'Six-fifty.'

Yes, he had known. He was testing her. 'So the arrangement for me to go down to the bay is off.' Cary spoke thoughtfully. He went back to the chapel and emerged with a torch. 'I can't even see any riding light.' He flashed the torch on, off, on, off.

'What are you doing?'

'Using the emergency signal.' He spoke absently, trying again. Still no answering flash came.

'Why did you need me to take you down to the cruiser, since you had it so well set up?'

'Your arrangement with Steve was to save a day.'

She remembered Scunthorpe saying that outside the Circe. 'How so?'

'They didn't know where I was. I had to come here every night at nine o'clock, and if *Venus* was here they would signal. But they must have been held up last night because you said they came in around midnight.'

'Yes.'

'I missed two nights, because I was too ill to walk this far.'

She looked up at him critically, and with hate. No wonder he had been in such a stew, cut off by illness from his escape route. That was why she had had to bring him all this way by donkey, on a roundabout route where he would not be seen because today he had to move by daylight. Up here, whatever happened, he could be in touch with *Venus*.

'So, as a result of my meeting those men, you could be on the cruiser and away by nine o'clock instead of up here, receiving the signal?'

'That's right. That's how it would have been if the police hadn't come. They would go back to sea leaving me with a day to clear up and get down to the bay.'

'And who,' she asked now, 'looked after Benjamin while you made the nine o'clock trek up here each night?'

'He was asleep.'

I hope he was, Alix thought angrily,

thinking of the terror of a small boy waking up alone in a dark house. She said: 'If the arrangement has been to signal at nine, how can you expect an answer now?'

'Someone might see it.'

'Why did you come here in the first place? Why didn't you fly straight to—North Africa?'

He swung round. Under his unblinking stare, she felt herself grow hot. She had so nearly said Tunis, and he had seen her hesitation. Cornered, Cary was as sharp as any fox. 'Where did you leave your handbag?' he asked, as though he guessed the truth.

'Sabri has it. I left as soon as I received your note. I simply threw the bag to him.'

She could tell he was pondering on the possibility of getting the telegram. Without it, all the tension and discomfort of the past two weeks would be wasted. 'You didn't say why—'

'It's the way things work,' Cary replied. He raised the torch and signalled again. 'I would be pretty obvious, hanging round a small North African town—especially with a child.'

'Why would you be "hanging around"?'

'I've a small business—'

'Arms.' She supplied the word flatly. 'Paul knows.'

'You don't like that, either.' His comment

was as inexpressive as hers had been. 'Damn! *Venus* came in. I saw her. What the devil is she doing? Even with your arrangement, they should be watching.'

'What happens when you get these guns? I mean, how do you get them?'

'I go over in *Venus* and signal off-shore. The boat comes out.'

'You deliver them personally?'

'We transfer again to another boat off-shore wherever the arms are sold.' He added coolly: 'No one sees me. So I am not known to the authorities at either end.'

'Did Dora know?' He was signalling again. 'I suppose she did,' Alix conjectured resignedly. 'She was here with you on your trips to Corfu.'

'She thought I went on business trips to Crete and Athens. She thought I was dealing in jute.'

'Was that her fatal error? Finding out?'

He did not reply and she had not expected him to. Of course it was too late and nothing would bring Dora back, but she wanted to know if he had even the smallest believable excuse for what he had done. 'Was it really an accident, Cary?'

'I don't want to talk about it.'

'I wish you would.'

He seemed to consider. Almost, she thought in surprise, as though he did want to get it off his chest. He signalled again, then

228

dropping the torch to his side, he gazed out over the moonlit hills and valleys, heaving an enormous sigh.

'Dora said—I'd had the opportunities. All those opportunities for making money and I'd—' he hesitated, then hurried over his excuse, '—things had gone wrong. She was pretty angry. It was going to mean a change in living standards for her. She didn't want to go abroad and be poor. But I knew she would go if it meant Marbella, or Capri, or some place like that. So I had to tell her about the arms.' He thrust his hands down into his pockets and stared broodingly out over the water. Alix turned with him. She could see his profile, but she could not see his eyes.

'She didn't like it?' Alix ventured.

'It wasn't that. It wasn't that at all. I am not making excuses for what I did, but you might be able to understand.' He turned and looked at Alix, adding in a queer, sad voice as though he saw years of loneliness stretching out ahead: 'She said, with all that money in Switzerland, I had to be the worst sort of failure to make a mess of things in London.'

Alix's mind flashed back to that party, to Cary, half-drunk on champagne, singing the song he had given to Dora, teaching the small Benjamin to sing it. Mommy's song.

*Sweet Lass of Richmond Hill*
*Sweet Lass of Richmond Hill...*

Yes, she thought then, with what was to be the least reaching out of sympathy to him, he had loved Dora. And she threw his failures in his face.

'I hit her,' said Cary. 'Just once. It only took one blow.' He added callously, bitterly: 'So, I hadn't the brains, but I did have the strength. She went down like a ninepin. I thought at first I'd knocked her out. I tried to revive her, I even gave her the kiss of life. But she was dead! It was no use calling a doctor, and if I told anyone, I would be arrested. I had to get away, but I needed time. I had to get the boy added to my passport. I hid her body in the culvert, and left.' He turned and looked down at Alix, his face totally expressionless. 'I've got to live with it now.'

'Cary, come back and give yourself up. You can't spend your life running away. Come back and tell your story. With good behaviour—'

He broke in excitedly: 'There's a riding light coming into view. It might be *Venus*.' He signalled again, and again, and again, and at last there came an answering flash.

'Right!'

'What is to happen?'

'They will come round and pick me up with the dory from the rocks below.'

'Thank heavens! Good luck, Cary,' Alix said softly. Sabri had said the cliff here was very steep. To her, it had looked vertical.

'I'll wait here until you're well away. Then I'll take Benjamin—'

'Sorry,' he interposed brusquely. 'Life is not as simple as that. You're coming with me.'

'Oh no!'

'Oh yes, I am afraid so. If you hadn't given me away to your friend Paul and the police, I would have gone off quite comfortably from the bay. But they've had time to get here now, and I need a hostage.'

'Cary!'

'Come on. We'll go down the track we came up and round the bottom. But you'll have to hurry.'

'Benjamin!' Her voice rose in a sort of panic. 'We can't leave him here.'

'We can, as a matter of fact,' retorted Cary callously.

'You vile, abominable man!'

'Yes, well, you knew that, didn't you! Come on.'

And then she remembered what there had been no time to recall before, the fact that Paul, when he returned to the Scheria, would get the note. She was certain he would follow to help her with Benjamin. Thank God the child was asleep. If he would only stay that way, Paul could find him. She said:

'Stop a moment. There are candles there. I'll light one and put it in the window.'

'We're short of time.'

'Not that short.' She broke away, ran to the chapel and tiptoed inside. A shaft of moonlight showed where the candles lay. There were matches. She lit one, held it to the wick and set the candle in a holder, then carried it to the cob-webbed window that faced the track.

'Hurry up.' She thought feverishly that Paul, if he was near, would see the flashlight. She would slow Cary down with every means available to her. They went in silence across the dry, stony ground and through the break in the wall. Here was the path winding steeply downhill. Cary gave her a rough shove. 'Get going.'

They both saw the light at the same moment. It was not far away. About a third, or a quarter of the distance to the road. Cary grabbed her by the shoulder, nearly pulling her off balance. He drew his gun, cocked it high and fired. The light went out. 'Okay,' said Cary, 'it's down the cliff. Come on. We've no time to waste now.'

# CHAPTER TWENTY-FOUR

Charles Hallow stood by while the Greek interrogated Sabri. These Greeks! Noisy devils! You'd think there was an instant row in progress. Perhaps they *were* having a row. A taxi pulled up in the road. A little old lady peered from the window. She had sharp blue eyes and her white hair was neatly set in corrugated waves. The driver took a stick from her and helped her to alight. She wore a shocking-pink dress, bright as the bougainvillaea. She stood for a moment surveying the scene with interest, then looked up and saw Hallow. She hobbled purposefully towards him.

'Didn't I see you on the plane?' she asked.

'Yes, I've just arrived.'

'You had more luck getting a taxi than I did, then. Where is the proprietor?' She leaned on her stick, looking round expectantly.

'This gentleman is the proprietor.' Hallow indicated Sabri.

She eyed him critically. 'I do seem to have come at an inopportune moment. Is something wrong?' Her gaze swept back to the guests, a sea of faces looking interestedly at the men.

'Excuse,' said Sabri, with an abrupt return

233

to business, side-stepping the inspector and meeting the new guest with charm and instant dignity. 'You want room?' He glanced down concernedly at the stick. 'I have only annexe. Lots of steps. Very steep.'

'I am Mrs Godfrey,' said Lucilla in her very precise voice. 'My niece, Mrs Johnston, is already here, so I shall be sharing her room.' Silence fell and she said, looking anxiously from one to another of the three astonished men: 'I was to come with my niece, but I was delayed. She is here, I presume?'

Hallow said: 'Would you care to sit down?'

Lucilla felt a cold hand close over her heart. 'What has happened to my niece?' she asked sharply. Sabri was busy ordering one of the waiters to bring a table and chairs to the paved terrace outside his office.

Hallow took her arm. 'Nothing has happened,' he replied, 'but I am afraid I haven't very good news.' The Greek inspector thrust a question at Sabri and he swung back, raising his arms, closing his eyes, screwing up his face, shouting his unintelligible reply: '*Ochi! Ochi!*'

'You are a policeman?' This man had the same formality and purposefulness Lucilla had seen in Mr Barrington.

'Yes, Detective Superintendent Hallow of Scotland Yard.'

'Are you here to catch Cary Johnston?' she asked bluntly.

'I am here by courtesy of the Corfu police. I gather you have seen the papers.'

'I know Dora Johnston's body has been found. That's why I am here. Well, not exactly that. I had a visit from a man called Barrington yesterday. No doubt you know him. I caught the first plane. I'd have come last night, but there is only one plane a day. You've come to arrest Cary?'

Hallow by-passed her question. 'Mrs Godfrey, it would appear that your niece has run off with Johnston. Does this surprise you?'

'Surprise?' echoed Lucilla, her face tightening distastefully. 'You don't know my niece, Mr Hallow.'

'She left a note saying so.'

'Frankly,' retorted Lucilla in her forthright way, 'I don't believe it.'

Hallow spoke to Sabri. 'Could you show Mrs Godfrey the note Mrs Johnston left?'

'No. Mr Crispin take it.' Sabri's black eyes flashed. 'I have hotel to look after. I do not care for politics.'

Hallow frowned at him. 'Hasn't the inspector explained? This man is a murderer.'

'Is not my affair.' Sabri sliced an arm forcefully through the air. 'I look after Missus Johnston because she is nice lady.

That is all.'

At the moment three Greeks in uniform with guns on their hips burst out of the darkness of the olive grove and ran across the road. A buzz of expectancy spread across the tables. There was a shout from one of the men in the group. Hallow leapt up from his chair, pointing out into the moonlit bay. 'Is that *Venus* coming round the point now?'

The Greek inspector said excitedly: '*Venus!* She's going up the coast!' He turned to Sabri and rattled off a deluge of Greek. Sabri shouted indignantly in return. The inspector said: 'If he wants to prove his innocence, he can take me out in his boat.'

'Is a tiny boat. Ski-boat.'

'All the better. It will be fast enough to catch that cruiser.'

Sabri looked angry and doubtful at one and the same time. 'I have business to run.'

Another noisy argument development. Lucilla said: 'What on earth is going on?'

'Your niece may be on that cruiser, Mrs Godfrey.'

Lucilla banged a fist down on the table. 'Then why isn't someone going after it?'

One of the men said: 'They didn't pick up anyone in the bay, according to the men at the Circe, but they could have pulled in to that far point on the way out.'

'You mean those signals might have been flashed to the point?'

'Maybe.'

Lucilla said indignantly: 'What are you great useless men doing standing here arguing? Why don't you get out that boat of yours and chase them?'

Sabri had heard that voice before. It belonged to his indomitable grandmother and he recognized it as representing a force for right that had disciplined his childhood and a good deal of his grown-up life. He said meekly: 'I get my boat.'

'All you have to do,' said Hallow, 'is fire a shot across the bow. I'll get over to the yacht bay and commandeer one of those bigger boats, if a couple of you chaps will come with me.'

One minute Lucilla was surrounded, the next she was on her own. She blinked in astonishment. An outburst like that at home would have evoked frigid silence. But there, Englishmen weren't likely to be standing around shouting at each other when there was something urgent to be done.

Sabri had rushed into his office bellowing orders, and the next moment a small boy dashed from behind the building with some clothes clutched to his breast. The other men scattered, some up the road and some to the beach. The turmoil over, Jane Langley looked narrowly across at the little old lady sitting alone with her suitcase beside her. In an odd, crumpled sort of way, she resembled

Alix. They had the same air of dignity and confidence. She rose and went over to her. 'Good evening,' she said diffidently. 'Are you, by any chance, Alix Johnston's aunt?'

The old lady looked up with a quick smile. 'Yes, I am. Do sit down.' As she moved towards Hallow's vacated chair, Sabri shot past running awkwardly like a worn teddy bear in jeans and a fisherman's sweater.

'I am Jane Langley. My husband has gone off to collect Cary Johnston's little boy.'

'He's here?' Lucilla's eyebrows shot up.

'Yes. There was a message saying that Alix and Cary had left him in the hills.'

'Alix left a little boy alone in the hills!' echoed Lucilla in disbelief. 'Rubbish!'

Jane said unhappily: 'I am afraid she—they—did. She left a note saying so.'

'I simply don't believe it,' retorted Lucilla flatly. 'Alix wouldn't do that. No woman would do that!' Jane nodded and she added: 'Especially Alix. And besides, where is the note? Everyone is talking about it, but no one seems to have it.'

'I don't know. Paul, the man who went off with my husband, said she left a note.'

'Yes, well, I'll believe it when I have seen it,' said Lucilla.

'She may be under his domination.'

'If she is, it would not be to that extent.' Their eyes met, and Jane nodded faintly.

'I am trying to think of an alternative.'

238

'If Alix has gone off with Cary, then she has gone against her will.'

'That's a bit frightening.'

A hundred yards away, faintly over the buzz of chatter, an engine burst to life. Some of the guests left their drinks and crossed the road, calling to each other. Several came via the terrace, deliberately, staring at Jane and Lucilla. A German from the scuba-diving school next door came up to Jane and said in impeccable English: 'What is happening? They are after that cruiser?'

'I think so.'

'Our caique is not very fast, but perhaps we could help. The boys have not been out today because of the wind.'

'Why don't you go down to the beach and ask?'

'Yes, I will.'

Jane said worriedly: 'I wish I knew what was happening. That cruiser isn't going out to sea. It's heading up the coast. My husband has gone to Castel Angelo to collect this child.' She stood up, fiddled with her belt, frowned. 'If you'll excuse me, Mrs Godfrey, I think I'll get in the car and go after him.'

'Can I come with you?'

Jane looked thoughtfully at Lucilla's bandaged ankle. 'It's kind of you, but the road only goes a certain distance, and then one has to walk over rough ground. I don't

239

even know where the track is, but I'll find the car. I wouldn't like to leave you in the wilds in a parked car.'

'And what are you going to do, my dear?'

'I don't know.' She added illogically: 'We've got four children. If there's any trouble, I'd like to be with my husband.' She had been more than a little unnerved by Mrs Godfrey's total certainty that Alix would not leave the child. Perhaps that mysterious note had been a trap to get Paul up to Castel Angelo. She ran across the paving stones and up the stairs to get the car keys.

Nico appeared from the dining terrace. 'You come to stay? You have booking?' He whistled and a boy came out of the kitchen door.

'I have come to join my niece, Mrs Johnston. May I be shown to her room?'

'Ah, yes.' He gave orders to the boy who picked up the bag, then said concernedly: 'Is steps.'

'Yes, but I dare say I can manage them slowly. Tell the boy to go ahead.'

She would not be greatly surprised if a bit of sun and sea water might not do this ankle at least as much good as the boring old lamp. Meantime, she would have a clean and tidy up, and then go back and keep an eye on things.

# CHAPTER TWENTY-FIVE

Brian switched off the flashlight as the shot rang out. 'My God! He's still there!' The two men dropped to the ground.

'Something has gone wrong,' said Paul in a shaken voice.

Were they both still here, and the child?

Brian said indignantly: 'A gun! Perhaps he has gone and left some Greek to cover for him.'

'Alix told me he had a gun.'

'You say that as though it's something everyone carries! What sort of people do you associate with?' the doctor asked distastefully.

'Not gunmen, if I can help it. But let's not waste our energy on being offended. Follow me.' They crawled into the shelter of some bushy trees.

'What do you suppose he's about? Holing up for a siege?'

'He killed his wife. Did you know they have found the body?'

'I saw it in the paper. But does Alix know?'

'She heard this afternoon.'

'And she has joined him?' Brian sucked his breath in noisily. 'I think, old chap, we had better go back and get the police.' He rose to his knees, then to a half-standing position, parting the light branches so that he had a view of the summit. From where they were, on a slope running into the shallow valley from which the peak of Castel Angelo rose almost perpendicularly, they could see no movement.

'The top is all ruined walls,' said Paul. 'He can shield himself with any number of stones. I dare say he thinks we are the police. Alix will have told him about their arrival.'

'So what are we going to do? He may not see me very clearly, if at all, in these dark clothes, but your light shirt will be pretty obvious. He is probably waiting to see if we turn back. Let's show willing before he starts worrying. He might aim a bit nearer next time.'

Paul's mind was sharpened by the danger. There was something about this situation that was beyond present comprehension but his brain had begun an attack. What if they had not been able to get away? Alix had told him about Cary's fever and the necessity to transport him by donkey because his legs were still too weak to walk. Could there have been a recurrence of the illness? Paul could not imagine Alix firing the gun—but then, he could not imagine her leaving the child, either. He had to re-think about that lovely lady.

'Hey!' he exclaimed excitedly. 'I think I've got it. Listen! Alix tells Johnston the police are here so there's no way now she and Cary can get on to the cruiser down in the bay—no, wait a minute. I've another idea! She had a good long start on us. She knew the time of the plane's arrival. She could have hired a boat. A small one. There are quite a lot of little outboards in the bay. Or she might have simply taken one and gone round to the foot of Castel Angelo. Sound carries at night. Cary would hear her, and see her too, in this bright moonlight. That could explain the bit about leaving the child. She might reckon that Johnston could climb down the cliff, but the boy wouldn't make it.'

'It's a theory,' returned the doctor without enthusiasm, 'but how would they transfer to the cruiser, since it is in the bay? And they know the police will make for Paleocastritsa.'

'It's only a sketchy sort of theory.'

'You're a jump ahead of me,' conceded Brian drily.

'It's my job to work things out and be one ahead of everyone else.'

'Then work this out. Why did Alix tell you all about Johnston, and where he was, and the arrangements with *Venus*, if she intended to run off with him?'

'I don't think she did, at that time. I think she poured it all out in a state of shock, and then walking back to the car, she must have had this sudden—what—impulse, and ran.

243

Jumped into a taxi, I suppose, and worked it out en route.'

'What you're saying is,' replied Brian, 'that she recovered from the shock, decided she wanted the man, and opted to accept him along with his nasty habits.'

'That's it.' Something like a knife twisted in Paul's stomach. 'A good five minutes must have passed since he banged out that shot. Would you be willing to swap your navy shirt for this light one?'

'What are you going to do?'

'I am going up to Castel Angelo.'

'You're mad!'

'Maybe.'

'No, I won't be a party to it. Come on. Let's start back and get the police. These Greeks are armed, and it's their job.'

'Okay, you go. And if I'm killed, you'll always have it on your mind that I was a good target in my cream shirt.'

'Really, Paul, you put me in an impossible position.'

Paul grinned to himself in the darkness of the tree's shadow. He was a past master at putting people in impossible positions when he needed to get his own way. 'Right, I'm off. Do you want the flashlight?'

'Hang on. I'll give you my shirt,' grumbled Brian. 'And take the flashlight. My eyes are quite accustomed to this light now. You're working on the theory he has gone, and the

244

boy is there alone?' He undid the buttons and slipped the shirt off.

'I'm working on half a dozen theories,' replied Paul, 'most of them pretty baseless, I'm afraid, but something might come out of them. Thanks for the shirt. And the flashlight. It may be useful when I get there. Take things carefully on the way back. The track is pretty rough.'

★      ★      ★

Cary said: 'Come on, let's get going, fast. They're holed up still, but they might be able to move from bush to bush without our seeing them. The police are trained to that sort of thing.'

'Cary, let me stay here. Please! If Benjamin wakes up he will be terrified.' She did not say that she was terrified herself. She had seen that cliff rising sheer and white from the water, hundreds of feet high, and then the bracken and scrubclothed summit treacherously shielding a drop perhaps as straight as the precipice below.

'He won't wake up. He sleeps like a log. Come *on!*'

He pushed her back across the flat summit, ignoring her protests. As they passed the chapel door she strained her ears for a sound from the sleeping child, but there was none. Half-hysterical with fright, she

245

was tempted to rush in and wake him. With Benjamin upset, there was the chance Cary would have to leave them both, but she could not risk it. He had shown too casual a disregard for his son's safety.

'Cary, he might wake. You'd never forgive yourself if he fell. The cliff is sheer, and he could easily—'

'Pack it in.' Cary gave her another push and she lost her balance. He grabbed her roughly and put her on her feet again.

In her anger and despair, she hit out at him, a wild slash that caught him on the forearm and may have hurt her more than it hurt him. His hand came up in a stinging blow across the side of her head. 'Let that be a lesson to you, cousin Alix. Get over there to the left.' Her head was reeling from the blow. She staggered, tripping on a stone. 'Look where you're stepping,' he said brusquely. 'You're not going to be much use to me if you fall head first down that cliff.'

Alix had never done any climbing. She fought against the terror but it caught in her throat, turned her stomach over and stiffened her joints. 'Have you had a good look at the cliff?' she asked savagely. 'You're mad, Cary! We haven't a hope of getting down it.'

'As a matter of fact, that's just what we have got. A hope, but not much more in this light. And it's thanks to you we have to do

246

it.' Cary thrust his stubbled face into hers, his eyes glaring, half-crazed in the cold moonlight. 'If you had exercised a little loyalty and kept your mouth shut you would not have been in this spot.' He dropped the flashlight into his pocket. His gun was in the other one. She had seen him put it there. 'Get going,' he said tersely, giving her another push. 'So long as no cloud comes over the moon at the wrong moment, and we keep our heads, we can do it. I've been here a few times, and I've had it in mind that something of this sort could happen. Turn now. Round that bit of wall. There's a very narrow path leading down steeply on the other side.'

'Cary! Stop before it's too late! You're going to kill us both. Come down the inner track. You could still make it. You've got your gun!'

She had swung round to face him. He grasped her brutally by the shoulders and swung her back. 'If you want some real persuasion, just say so. We're nowhere near the cliff proper yet. We've got to get down through this scrub.'

From where she stood now, beyond the broken wall, she could see the water like feathered glass below. She hated heights and her head was swimming with fear. There was plenty of dry scrub, tough and useful as a hand-hold, but deceiving as to the shape of the decline. She edged forward gingerly. The ground beneath the scrub was rock-hard with loose stones that slid away easily, frighteningly, from beneath her flat rope soles. She slid forward and came up against a root.

'Get on!' rasped Cary impatiently.

She edged forward again, sliding one foot, feeling for foot-holds with her toes. The bank fell away here. Over on the right a yawning abyss with the cold starlight shining down on spray-whitened rocks hundreds of feet below. She stopped and stared, fascinated, horrified, feeling herself drawn dizzily towards the edge, drawn to what seemed like inevitability and a mindless desire for release from the untenable fear that racked her. From the madman only inches away.

'Get on,' said Cary. 'I don't want to push you. But we can't spend the whole night here while you make up your mind whether you can do it or not.'

Alix took a deep breath and leaning over, grasped the twisted stem of a tiny scrub tree. She clung there, allowing her feet to slide a little. They struck a moss-grown rock and she was loosening her grip on the rough hand-hold when suddenly the rock gave way with a rattle and shush of falling scree. Her hands tightened convulsively as she shot over the edge, scraping her back agonizingly on the stones. There was a straining at her arm muscles and then a painful jerk as she stopped. Her feet, groping for a foot-hold, flailed in nothingness.

Cary said in a cool, businesslike voice: 'Hang on. I'll go down this way and see if I can pull you over. I dare say the scrub would break your fall if you let yourself go, but you'd better not take a chance.'

Her teeth were gritted against the pain in her arms and she needed all her strength to hold on. She closed her eyes to block out the stars glittering coldly through the snow-pondering of the Milky Way. She could hear Cary feeling his way down the pebbled slope close by, hear the rattle of stones as he dislodged them, the crack of breaking twigs. Her mind flew hysterically back up the mountain to little Benjamin: God! Let him sleep until he is found. To Aunt Lucilla in London, worrying, fuming: Don't weep for me. Perhaps, after Tim, it had to be like this. To Paul: Help me. Somehow, know, and come.

An age later, Cary's voice came up from below. 'All right. You can let go and slide. There's a hole here and I am standing below it on a ledge. Let go. You can't go wrong.'

Alix released her numb fingers and shot down a dizzy drop to land in a heap at Cary's feet. 'I'll go in front now,' he said, adding with satisfaction: 'There's not much chance of your getting up there at a run.' Sick with fear, she looked back, and then down. They seemed to be stuck on a ferny ledge between the sky and the sea. He was right, she could never get back, but neither did she feel she could go on. Her back had been scraped raw on the hard stones and her hands were bleeding, but that was nothing to the sheer blind horror of what was in front.

'Come on,' said Cary through his teeth. There was a sort of excitement pounding through his anger now. Alix shrank away from him, half sobbing with terror.

'I can't. My legs are trembling. I can't do it, Cary. Please go on without me.' Huddled at his feet, she looked up at him. 'Are you trying to kill me—this way?' she whispered.

He seemed to take stock, calm a little. He seemed to be assessing her worth, dead or alive. Then unexpectedly, he said: 'You'll survive the night, if you keep your head. And if the police aren't too trigger-happy. You're in no danger from me. Why should you be? All I want is a shield from any bullet meant for me. Come on, Alix. Let's get going again.' He turned round, then gave an exclamation of triumph. '*Venus* is coming round the heads!' And there she was, a tiny craft moving silkily towards them through the choppy water, her bow and starboard lights gleaming, the wash fanning away, pearl white, from the stern. Cary drew his flashlight out of his pocket and flashed it. They waited and at last came an answering signal. 'Ah!' said Cary exultantly. 'It's nearly over.'

The cruiser came on silently towards them. Beyond the point, a little string of fishing caiques were drifting directly out to sea, their carbide lamps glowing gold on the water.

Alix looked down on the cruiser with naked fear. 'Cary! You're not going to take me aboard!'

'We'll see. Get moving. Are you going to follow me, or shall I push you along in front? It's up to you.'

'I'll follow,' she promised. There seemed no point in fighting. She was not going to survive this break-neck cliff, and nor was he. It was nearly over.

She hoped only that the end would not be too painful, too drawn-out.

'Well, do that. One false move, and I warn you...'

'There's no need. I will follow.' Acceptance. The end.

'We're going over to the right here,' Cary said. 'We'll have to get on to the cliff proper now. There is a bit of a spur and then the bank juts out where there was a landslide. If we take it carefully, we ought to be all right.' Cary began to let himself down, hand over hand, and Alix followed.

251

Since her acceptance of what was to come, her mind had atrophied. There was no future except the torture of the climb and soon it would be over. They went on down, hand over hand, slipping, bumping up against a root or stone, then moving on. Alix's forearms were scraped, her elbows raw.

Cary said: 'Stop. This is where we go out on the open cliff. There's not much to hold on to here, but the rock should be firmer than this stuff under the scrub.'

Alix looked down over the naked precipice, white in the moonlight, and suddenly came alive again with a cry of sheer terror.

Or thought she did. Then she realized she had not opened her mouth, but a cry had come. The terrified scream of a child.

## CHAPTER TWENTY-SIX

Cary slapped a hand over her mouth. She struggled to free herself, not knowing whether she was going to shout or not, then suddenly Cary exclaimed in a low, incredulous voice: 'Jesus!' and let her go. She looked up and there was Benjamin's tiny figure, poised like a bird, high above them on the cliff top, looking down.

'Wait for me!' came the sobbing cry and

the little boy moved forward.

'Stop!' Cary's explosive shout was too late. They could see Benjamin's slim form hurtling through the bushes that masked the treacherously steep bank; a high-pitched shriek; the scramble and thump that was a crazy whirling of the small body over and through the bushes; the rattle of an avalanche of stones. Then nothing. A breathless silence. Then, a whimpering cry: 'Daddy!'

'Don't move!' Alix and Cary shouted the words in unison, but if Benjamin heard he was too intent on getting to his father to obey. They saw him fling himself upright among the tough little bushes that had broken his fall, overbalance in a flailing of arms and dive forward again to toss over and down the near-vertical slope. Alix never knew how long the noise of Benjamin's coming beat against her senses; her heart seemed to stop, waiting for his final plunge to death. There was nothing she could do. Nothing Cary could do. They stood in an airless, lifeless vacuum as the small body topped past them. Or seemed to stand. Afterwards, Alix knew that she had leaped towards him, grasped at air and felt the brush of his departure as he went over the cliff. Then she could not think any more. Could not see. Could not look. She shrank into the cliff face, thinking: We're all losers, in a way. But Benjamin never had a chance.

\*　　　\*　　　\*

Paul was coming warily over the abutment when he heard the child's scream. He leaped out from behind the grey stones and ran forward across the dry grass in the ghostly moonlight. There were two donkeys, jerking at their ropes, leaping uselessly with fright. The scream came again. He changed direction, still running, and jumped down a bank between some old retaining walls, then stopped dead, his blood freezing in his veins. Beyond the first dark drop where the sturdy mountain plants grew, there was a sloping shelf where the cliff broke in. A landslide had removed a portion of the mountain and the fallen rocks, stones and soil had hardened into a shoulder and thrust out from the cliff. The child had gone over and was lying there, not far down, on a ledge.

Paul slid down the steep slope, grasping at tough heather and small, hard plants. Slipping and slithering, he made his way down as fast as an element of safety would allow. He had plenty of experience of mountain climbing and his muscles were strong, his movements quick but sure. He slithered boldly as Cary and Alix had not been able to do because he knew what to look for, what bushes were strong, how to zig-zag, how to ricochet in leaps from one foot-hold that might take his weight for only the second he needed, to another that would hold him for long enough to check his course. He did not look at the sea glimmering up in the moonlight far below, he did not think of the boy. He had his mind on movement, judging distances, testing strengths, his own and that of the rocks and the friendly flora, doing a job coolly and with calm courage the way he always did these things.

Cary said: 'He's stuck on a ledge about twelve feet down.'

Alix heard him but she did not take in the words.

'He's all right,' said Cary. 'He's looking up.'

She heard him then, but she did not believe him. Benjamin could not be alive. She could imagine how it was over the edge, his small broken body, the dead face upturned. She stayed frozen where she was, looking at nothing. There were noises round her, too, somewhere above, but they did not mean anything. They were part of the turbulent morass of immediate disaster that held her paralysed. Then Cary said: 'I'm going down. I think I can reach him, but I don't know how I'll get him up. If he will keep still...'

Cary's words broke through the wall Alix

had erected in her mind, startling her back from creeping nothingness into the horror of the present. She saw Cary remove his jacket and going down on hands and knees, test the edge. She moved forward in wonder, time suspended as she peered over, and there was Benjamin looking up at her, his face as white as the cliff itself, blank, shocked, staring. He was on a narrow ledge supported by a tree stump growing nearly horizontally with the roots like a black sea creature clawing at the cliff. The upper part of the tree was long since gone, the roots had died, starved when the cliff soil eroded round them, but a small ledge of rock and clay soil and grasses had remained, or even built up from debris coming from above, like an abandoned, broken eagle's eyrie.

Alix heard her own voice, and marvelled at its sweet calm, marvelled at the words that came from her own lips. 'Hallo, Benjamin. Get you, down there!' He did not answer. As though aware his life hung by a thread, he went on staring, utterly immobile. She was scarcely aware of Cary going over the edge. She said to Benjamin: 'Don't move. So long as you don't move we'll get you up.'

Cary said: 'There's nothing to hold on to. It's sheer.' He came back and sat down on the rough stones. The child went on staring, unblinkingly. Alix thought: We can't get him without a rope, and there isn't time. He'll move, and go. The noise above grew louder, somehow like thunder, or rain or just a thumping in her mind. Then her mind stopped playing tricks and she knew it was someone coming down the cliff, for there was the shower of stones sweeping through the brush behind them. They both turned.

Paul said: 'You!' incredulously.

Without acknowledging Paul's arrival, Cary said: 'If you could hold my hands so I could slide slowly on my front, I could get to him and wait with him until you get a rope. Are you strong enough to hold me?'

'Yes,' said Paul. No more than that.

Cary knelt at the edge with his back to the sea. Alix looked down and smiled. 'Daddy's coming,' she said softly. 'Don't move, darling.' She knew the water was down below, and the rocks, but she did not see them now. The dizziness had gone, the fright, the sickness. She smiled calmly down at the silent child like a nurse watching over a helpless patient. She knew afterwards the calm was a cloak to mask an untenable, unbearable panic too great to contain. A gift to carry her through.

Cary went over the edge. Paul had chosen a spot where a small rock thrust up a few inches in the soil. He lay flat against it, stretched out, and as Cary eased himself over he made ready to take Cary's hands. Alix knelt down and grasped Paul's ankles. Paul edged nearer the cliff top. His muscles tightened as he took Cary's weight, then Cary said: 'I have a foot-hold now. You can let go.'

They stood up and moved in silence to the edge. Cary was stuck like a fly on a wall. His foot-hold must have been small for they could not see it. Benjamin had not moved. He was still staring up. Cary had gone down a little to the right of him. Paul said: 'If you move your left leg out about a foot and slide it down, there is a bit of a ledge, but I can't see if it is rock or not.' They watched him edge across. His left hand had found a jutting flange. His foot inched along and down. He tested the foot-hold once, twice, then lowered himself until it took his full weight. 'I think I'll make it now,' he said. 'It's rougher here. Holes.' From above, they could not see the shape of the cliff. They watched in silence, and a moment later he was there. Benjamin looked up as Cary looked down at him. 'I knew you'd come, Daddy,' he said.

Cary did not answer. Perhaps he could not. He stood there gazing down and suddenly Alix realized he was not looking at the child. He was looking at the rough structure on which they stood. Then he said hoarsely: 'It's not going to hold.' Quick as a flash, he had Benjamin under the arms, jerking him above his own shoulders. 'Lean down and take him.' There was not time or breath to say: Quickly! but Paul felt the thrusting urgency in Cary's voice and dropped flat again.

'Hold my feet!' Alix leaped back and grasped him round the ankles. She felt him edging away and went with him, inch by inch, her fingers tightening convulsively. Then Paul said: 'Pull!' She dragged at his ankles, but he was a big man and she could not pull him back. Teeth gritted, breath held, her muscles clamped, she tugged with every ounce of strength in her, then he twisted, his legs jack-knifed and she lost her grip. She swung up in a panic, a scream in her throat, and there was Benjamin's head and shoulders, and Paul, gripping him, but because of his awkward position, unable to exert sufficient force to pull him over the top.

She leaped forward, grabbed the child by one arm and jerked him brutally to safety. Benjamin skidded across the rough ledge, head first. There was a crack like a pistol shot, a scream from Cary and she looked down to see the old tree stump pull away, its tentacles jerking from the cliff face, and the precarious little spur that had been strong enough for the small child, but not for the man, give way in a horrifying rush of stones and rock and soil and wood. She saw Cary's arms flail the air like the wings of a long, sad bird, saw his ravaged, horrified face, and for the very last time, she saw Tim's eyes, as he lurched over backwards, dropping helplessly into the abyss below. At the last he screamed again. A long, shuddering scream that rent the air and was lifted on the wind to drift to nothingness across the silent sea.

Benjamin heard it. Clambering to his knees, his face buttoned up against the pain of his grazed limbs, he checked his own cry of anguish. Alix turned, swept him into her arms and pressed his face against her shoulder. 'Thank God you're safe.'

Paul was lying flat still. He twisted into a sitting position and put an arm across his eyes.

'Where's Daddy?'

That same strange, God-gifted remedial calm took hold of her again. 'He had to go down. He'll be all right,' she said soothingly.

'Down where?' Benjamin asked suspiciously, his eyes overbright, his mouth tightening.

'Downwards. It was easier for him to go down. We won't see him for a while.'

'I heard him scream.'

'Shout,' she corrected him. 'He was shouting to the people down there. He has gone to them, but we have to go back the way we came because it's easier for us to do that. Daddy will go back in the boat.'

Paul looked at her, his face a study. She met his eyes without seeing them. She was thinking that Cary, against all the odds, had died saving the life of the son he had treated so badly. You never did know about human beings. And Dora? A life for a life. You never did know about Fate.

Paul rose, went to the edge and looked down. '*Venus* is there,' he said.

Her mission unfulfilled.

'And, well, that's an odd one—the caique that belongs to the German scuba divers! It's following. And a motor boat. Could be Sabri's. It's like the one they use for water ski-ing.' He drew a long, weary breath. 'I'd say they had things tied up.' He went on staring down at the water far below.

Benjamin's arms went round Alix's neck. 'I was scared.'

'Yes, darling, but it's all over now. We're going home.' She stiffened, waiting for him to say: 'To Mommy?' but he only replied : 'I was scared when I waked up. *And* when I fell over the bank. And I hurt myself.'

Paul said: 'Brian went back for help. Shall I get him? Or do you think you could make it back to the top, with me to assist?'

Alix looked up at the frowning peak, the scarred cliff, furred with the mountain growth that had helped her down. It was not as bad as the one below, not nearly as bad. It was negotiable, for someone who was strong and wary and in his right mind. But it was more than she could face now. Her legs were shaking. She sat down on a jutting rock with Benjamin on her knees. 'No. I can't make it.'

'I'll get Brian, and a rope.' Paul moved a few steps away, then turned back. 'I'm sorry,' he said.

She did not answer. She supposed he was thinking of Cary as a loss of sorts. She could not think about him at all, now, and she did not want to. When there is nothing good to remember, it is time to forget. Eventually, Benjamin would know his father saved his life and perhaps by then, she would be able to filter that star from the pitch darkness, and remember too.

Paul moved off, his feet brushing noisily in a patch of shale. There was something about his going that she could not stand. It was as though he swept a great scar of conscious loneliness and emptiness across his wake. A cloud touched the moon and the world darkened, frighteningly. Cary was no longer gone. He was a broken body at the cliff base and his ghost was all around.

'Wait for me,' she cried into the stark silence.

Paul turned, but he did not come back. His waiting was a duty, a security, without the living pulse of warmth. 'Are you sure you can make it?' he asked formally, as though speaking to a stranger. 'I'll take him, of course.'

'If you will help.' She hadn't much

262

strength left. She had been climbing and hurrying and rebounding from shocks for eighteen hours. Her real strength had gone long since but the nervous energy, too insubstantial to trust, still came in spurts and she reckoned it would get her through, with Paul's help.

'Of course,' he said again. He looked across at her. The cloud had cleared the moon and he could see what the day had done to her. He spoke more gently: 'We don't need to go straight up, anyway. We may be able to find a way along here and back into the valley. It will take a lot longer, but...'

'There's time,' she said dully. 'Let's go.'

## CHAPTER TWENTY-SEVEN

Tonight it was the Calypso's turn for Greek dancing, but nobody moved from the Scheria. Dinner was served in a buzz of excitement. The guests had witnessed the arrival of the police, the drama of Sabri's quick change from dapper black and white to fisherman's garb; they had witnessed his precipitate abandonment of his dining-room duties. They had heard that extraordinary outburst from the attractive young Englishman who had walked blindly into a taxi, the rush to the beach of a little crowd of excited Germans from the scuba-diving school next door, pulling on their waterproofs as they ran, and then the departure of their caique. A yacht had crossed between the twin heads and disappeared. Several people swore they had heard a shot fired. On top of all this, the pretty English girl had gone. Then someone announced that the English doctor had left and his wife, who had seemed so quiet and respectable, had been seen racing across the terrace and roaring away in their car. The waiters, when asked, seemed to have lost their tenuous hold on the English language.

Lucilla Godfrey had asked Nico for a table near the entrance. She had had little appetite until she saw the lush cucumber and tomato salads with their fat black olives, and smelled the intoxicating aroma of the Greek menu. She tucked swiftly into a plate of mince and rice wrapped intriguingly in vine leaves, but her mind was elsewhere. Afterwards, she settled down at a tiny table beneath a palm that gave a good view of the beach as well as the road.

It must have been two hours before there was the sound of an engine drumming in from the sea and tiny red and green lights appeared below the monastery. The guests rose en masse from their seats and in a clatter of excitement and conjecture, hurried across the road to the beach. A ghostly yacht appeared, passing between the heads, and moving on round the bay. Then the Germans' caique came in, its engine throbbing through the silence of the night-still water, cut, and slid silently in to the beach.

Lucilla found she could not rise from her seat to follow the crowd. She sat alone at her table waiting while the guests surged excitedly past her. If the three craft she knew to be concerned, had all returned, then presumably Alix was there, safe, and would appear in due course. Nico came and stood before her. He did not speak, but he smiled reassuringly. Lucilla said: 'I think I would like a brandy.'

'Brandy? Yes.' Nico turned to go, then hesitated. A car was approaching. It pulled up outside the hotel and there was Alix, white-faced, with a child in her arms. Lucilla gaped, then turned to Nico. 'Two brandies, please, young man.'

Through the open window Alix heard that very distinctive voice. She looked up, and two tears slid down her cheeks. Lucilla rose from the table and hobbled forward as the driver helped Alix out of the car. 'Well, my dear,' she said, 'I expected you by boat.'

'Oh!' said Jane faintly. 'I forgot to tell you, your aunt is here.'

They kissed, and then Lucilla said: 'I'd

265

suggest you go straight to your room. This is Benjamin?' She looked down at the sleeping child in Alix's arms. Alix nodded. 'And Cary?'

'Johnston is dead,' said Brian. 'I am a doctor. We need to get these two to bed.'

'Nico!' said Lucilla, in a voice of command, 'I would be glad if you would remove my things from Mrs Johnston's room and put them in the annexe. Don't trouble with the brandy now.'

They moved across the terrace. Suddenly, there was an exultant shout: 'Missus Johnston! You are well?'

Alix turned, smiling. Sabri was bounding across the road, a squat little man in black fisherman's cap and old clothes. 'Quite well, thank you, Sabri.'

'Where is the scooter?'

'Mr Crispin is riding it back.'

Sabri shook his head, puzzled, then a smile spread over his brown features, and he patted her arm. The guests had begun to trail back from the beach. Alix went up the steps with the sleeping child, Nico hurrying ahead with the key and Lucilla, with Brian's help, coming behind.

They slipped Benjamin's clothes off and put him between the sheets. 'Do you think you'll sleep?' asked Brian worriedly. 'I wish I had a sedative for you.'

Alix said wanly: 'I don't think I'll need it.'

She gave Lucilla a brief summary of what had occurred but before she came to the end sleep was sweeping over her like an aching tide. Lucilla went quietly out of the door and made her way back down the stairs. Most of the guests had drifted off. The hotel, tucked cosily into its hill with the little coloured lights peering out of vines, looked glamorous and tranquil and safe. Thank goodness Alix was all right. Lucilla would sleep peacefully now. She was not going to admit to being too old for junketing round the world, but she did feel her age when she had to do it under pressure and without sleep. She looked round for Nico but he had disappeared. A Lambretta leaned up against a tree on the opposite side of the road and a good-looking young man sat alone at one of the tables. He had two glasses in front of him. He's found my order, thought Lucilla good-naturedly, and smiled at him. He rose courteously. 'Would you care to join me in a night cap?'

At seventy-plus, thought Lucilla, amused, such offers were not so frequent that they might be turned down. She hobbled over and he drew out a chair. 'Did you find these?' she asked pointing to the brandy glasses.

'I ordered them. It's a night for doubles. What will you drink? I am Paul Crispin.'

'I'm Lucilla Godfrey, and being old

enough to be at least your mother, if not your grandmother, may I suggest you give me one of those?'

Paul grinned. 'You're Alix's aunt?'

'Ah! You know her?'

Paul? The man who had gone on the bike to find someone to bring the donkeys down?

'Not very well,' replied Paul sardonically. 'She is the reason I was drinking two brandies alone. Tell me, Mrs Godfrey, were you aware of this—er—tie?' his mouth turned down bitterly, 'between Alix and Cary Johnston?'

'There wasn't one,' said Lucilla flatly. 'I've already been asked this once tonight. I cannot imagine how the rumour started. The poor girl has been through the most ghastly experience during the past few days, at Cary's hands.'

'Did you not know she planned to run away with him tonight?'

'Balderdash!' said Lucilla.

'She left a note.'

Lucilla smiled grimly. 'Yes, I've heard about that note, but the funny thing is, no one seems able to produce it.'

Paul reached into his pocket and brought out a very crumpled piece of paper. He smoothed it and laid it on the table between them. 'There's your proof.'

Lucilla reached into her handbag and drew out her spectacles. 'That,' she said authoritatively, 'is not Alix's handwriting.'

Paul stared at her.

'It is the note Cary sent to her to trick her into going up that mountain.' She read it aloud. '"*Gone. Left B.*"—the child—"*C. A.*"—that's the mountain. "*Thanks.*" Well,' she commented acidly, 'at least he had the grace to thank her for her misguided efforts. How did you come by this, young man?'

'She left it for me.'

'To tell you where she had gone, and why.' Lucilla gave him a cool look. 'Without mincing words,' she said, 'for such an intelligent looking young man, you jump to some pretty unintelligent conclusions.'

⋆     ⋆     ⋆

It was mid-day before Alix wakened. She stretched, yawned, stared contentedly at the ceiling, then as memory crept towards her in a dark cloud, she shut her eyes, trying to push everything out. Cary ... Dora ... The police ... Paul ... Benjamin—she shot to a sitting position, blinking across at the empty twin bed. Where was Benjamin? She flung the bedclothes away, put her feet to the floor and slid over to the bathroom. Empty! She ran to the door and there was Paul, leaning back in a deckchair, eyes closed against the sun. She flung her wrap round her, opened the door and called in a high, nervous voice:

'Paul! Where is Benjamin?'

He shot upright, then came towards her, smiling. 'He is on the beach with your aunt. So you have wakened at last! Are you ready for a swim?'

She stepped back inside, feeling dazed. She did not know what to make of his friendliness, after last night. Or was it mere politeness? She went into the bathroom and threw some water on her face. Now that she was properly awake, she ached in every limb. Her right heel was stabbingly painful. She ran a comb through her hair and looking in the mirror saw there was a red weal on her right cheekbone. Her hands were cut, too, and there were raw patches right along her forearms. She sat down on the side of her tiny sit-up bath, contemplating her wounds. Why was Paul sitting outside her room? Had the police sent him? They were bound to want to interview her. What a mess! she thought grimly. She was not even clean. Didn't I have a wash last night? She could not remember. Brian and Lucilla had been urging her into bed and the main consideration had been trying not to wake Benjamin.

Her bikini was over the towel rail. She pulled it on. There was an enormous black bruise on one shoulder, and one on each arm where Cary had grabbed her, torturing her into telling him she knew about Dora. Her feet were swollen, and the painful split blister looked ugly. She did not want to go down to the beach like this. She went into the bedroom and lay dejectedly on the bed, eyes closed.

Paul looked in the door and saw her. His heart sank. Did that hard-hitting, blunt old Yorkshire woman really know what made her niece tick? He said uncertainly: 'Alix?'

She opened her eyes and looked at him. 'All right,' she said, her voice trembling, 'I treated you badly, but I had a job to do. Thank you for bringing us out of it. I'd have thanked you last night if you hadn't shot off the way you did.' If you hadn't been so cold, she wanted to say, so distant, and uncaring. If you had not treated me like a bit of wood. She felt the tears coming and turned away, closing her eyes.

Paul came nervously into the room and stood looking down at her. He saw the black bruises and the weals and grazes, and the dirt. 'Just one thing,' he said in a subdued, even, waiting voice. 'Were you, or were you not in love with Cary?'

'No.'

'Were you going away with him?'

'As a hostage. He tricked me into going back. You saw the note.'

'Yes,' he said contritely, 'I saw the note. Forgive me. I thought it was from you—to me.' He sat down on the bed. 'I thought you were telling me you had left Benjamin at Castel Angelo. I went up to collect him—and found you.'

'Lord!' said Alix. She put her hand over her eyes. Then she started to laugh. She laughed weakly and continuously, as though she was crying.

A key turned in the door and Lucilla walked in with Benjamin. 'Hallo,' she said cheerfully, 'I thought it was time for you to wake up.'

'Sorry about your bed, Lucilla. Where did you sleep?'

'In the annexe. It's up the cliff a bit and the steps are steep, but it's a challenge. A kind Frenchwoman I have been talking to is going into Corfu, and she is going to get Benjamin a bucket and spade. Very concerned about you, she was, dear.'

'Oh, you lazybones!' exclaimed Benjamin, 'I been on the beach for hours. You—in bed in your bikini!'

'We're going swimming.'

'I'll get into my trunks.' Paul made for the door.

'Come on, Aunt Lucilla. I'm going to show her where the hermit crabs are,' Benjamin told Alix.

'It's a rough track,' said Alix warningly.

Lucilla grimaced. 'I dare say I'll cope. I say, this child sings like an angel! And by the way, I've talked to the police and sent them on their way. I've told them they're not to bother you, that you will get in touch when you're able.'

'Thanks, Lucilla.' Alix sat up and put her feet to the floor. 'It was good of you to come. Ouch.'

'I wouldn't have missed it for anything. And that nice Dr Langley agrees with me that the salt water could do my ankle a lot of good.'

★    ★    ★

Alix and Paul swam out together to the rocks opposite the monastery. The water was clear as glass again. When they grew tired they climbed up on the rocks and put their masks and flippers behind them. The sky was cloudless and the wind moved in caressingly from the north. Beyond the tranquil monastery with its orange tiles and green sentinel cypresses reared the great spur of Castel Angelo with its tiny chapel glinting like a square pearl in the sun. Alix said: 'I want to tell you the whole story, from the beginning.'

'Don't. Don't go through it again.'

'I have to exorcise it.' And she had to do it here, where the gentle breeze would puff the ghosts away. She started with Tim, because that was where it all began, 'They look alike,' she ended. 'In some strange, inexplicable
273

way, though they were so different they resembled each other.' And then, wonderingly, she spoke a thought aloud. 'They weren't different,' she said, 'after all.' They were spendthrifts and failures, both. Odd, how she had missed that. She had only been aware, until this moment, that they had the same eyes. She turned to Paul. 'I'm glad I told you. I've exorcised more than I knew was there.'

He lifted her hand and held it on his knee. 'Did you know there is a resemblance between you and Dora? That's why I thought she was you. I had a photograph.'

'In a way. We're much the same type. I suppose the boys had the same taste. It's all part of the story.'

Across the turquoise inlet came a peal of bells from the monastery of the Virgin Mary. 'I shall never forget Corfu,' said Alix softly. 'In spite of what happened. And I shall always be grateful to St. Spiridon who gave me my wish. That day you found me in his church, I had asked him to save Benjamin.'

Paul gave her a whimsical smile: 'He's quite a boy, Spiridon.'

'He is indeed. I've got a card with a list of his miracles. An old woman at the door of his church gave it to me. Only I can't read it. It's in Greek. Perhaps I'll apply to have Benjamin's miracle tacked on the end.'

He laughed. 'What was it you said about

Corfu? "A landscape which precipitates the inward crisis of lives as yet not fully worked out." I understand that now, Alix.' His own life had been ready for reassessment.

'I feel free now,' she said. 'I feel I can start again. A new life.'

'It's been a rough sort of baptism,' he said sympathetically. 'I'll have to go back today or tomorrow. What will you do?'

'I must get in touch with Dora's parents. I am in their hands. They will want Benjamin, I dare say.'

'Will you ring me, when you're free?'

Free? She smiled at him. The freedom was within. It had nothing to do with family duties. 'I'll ring,' she said.